"That was your first kiss?"

"Aye, and my last, I expect. Once I go back to St. Gabriel, the monks will keep me away from future visitors."

"Go back! You would go back there to live in such isolation?"

"It's all I've ever known," Bridget said. "The monks are my family."

"But you are a lovely young woman. You should be meeting young men who will court you and offer you a life and a family of your own. You should be having a *real* first kiss and many more."

She smiled. "It was real enough."

"Nay, it was not. A real kiss is not a fumbled gesture in the dark between strangers. It's an expression two people use when their hearts are too full to express their love any other way."

Her eyes misted. "'Tis something I'll never have, then."

He raised a finger and wiped a tear that had started down her cheek. "Aye, you will, angel," he said. Then he lowered his lips to hers....

Praise for Ana Seymour's recent titles

Lord of Lyonsbridge
"…wonderful characters…a highly enjoyable read."
—*Romantic Times Magazine*

A Family for Carter Jones
"…a deliciously sweet tale of love."
—*Wichita Falls Times Record News*

Jeb Hunter's Bride
"…a brilliant historical romance."
—*Affaire de Coeur*

Maid of Midnight
Harlequin Historical #540—December 2000

Ana Seymour

Maid of Midnight

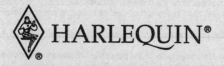

HARLEQUIN®

TORONTO • NEW YORK • LONDON
AMSTERDAM • PARIS • SYDNEY • HAMBURG
STOCKHOLM • ATHENS • TOKYO • MILAN • MADRID
PRAGUE • WARSAW • BUDAPEST • AUCKLAND

ISBN 0-373-29140-X

MAID OF MIDNIGHT

Available from Harlequin Historicals and
ANA SEYMOUR

Please address questions and book requests to:
Harlequin Reader Service
U.S.: 3010 Walden Ave., P.O. Box 1325, Buffalo, NY 14269
Canadian: P.O. Box 609, Fort Erie, Ont. L2A 5X3

For my sister, Barbara Jackowell, with much love and thanks for all your encouragement, ideas, research…and for setting me on the path to a medieval monastery!

Chapter One

It felt good to be mounted on Thunder again after the rough Channel crossing. Ranulf grimaced as he remembered the endless swells and how close he had come to the indignity of losing the contents of his stomach.

This was better. He took a deep breath of crisp spring air. The Norman countryside was lushly green. A pretty brown thrush burst suddenly out of a gorse bush just ahead of him.

Ranulf smiled. His grandmother Ellen had always said that her Normandy homeland was the loveliest place on earth, outside of Lyonsbridge. He'd visited here once before, coming home from the Crusades, but he'd been traveling with an army in chaos after the capture of King Richard. There had been little time to admire the scenery.

There would be little time this trip, either, he

thought, his smile fading. He was not here for pleasure. He'd come to find Dragon. And he didn't intend to return to the warmth and comfort of Lyonsbridge until he could ride there with Dragon at his side.

He knew that the others counted his younger brother as dead. Two long years had passed without word. His grandmother had secretly ordered the holy brothers to begin masses for Edmund's soul. But Ranulf refused to believe that his brother, a fighter so fierce he'd earned the name Dragonslayer, was dead. He *would* find him, no matter how long it took. He'd search every corner of this bloody continent, even if it meant riding all the way to Jerusalem.

He intended to start with an obscure little abbey called St. Gabriel.

Bridget clucked her tongue in reproof as Brother Francis presented her yet another habit with the hem shredded like cabbage.

"If you all insist on continuing your tinkerings, we'll not have a garment left to clothe you," she said, shaking her head.

Francis's round cheeks dimpled. "Now that would be a sight if the bishop ever did get around to visiting us here. A bunch of naked monks, being ordered about by a girl."

Bridget forced her face into a frown, but her eyes danced. "Careful, Brother Francis, lest you have to do penance for such talk." The frown turned genuine. "Who says I order you about?"

The plump little monk looked as if he wanted to put an arm around her shoulders, but he stopped himself and said instead, "Ah, child, let's call it *directing,* not ordering. And well you know that half the brotherhood would perish without you to care for us."

Bridget smiled. "I'll admit to wondering at times how you all managed before I came along."

"The Lord sent you to us. 'Tis the only answer. We've pondered it these many years since the day—"

Bridget waited, but she knew that Brother Francis would speak no further about her mysterious appearance at the abbey years ago. It had been her home as long as she could remember, but even now that she was a woman grown, the monks refused to speak of how she had gotten there.

She had stopped asking. It was enough that the monks loved her and she them. Though she'd devoured the abbey books on life outside the secluded monastery, she was happy here. She enjoyed her overflowing garden, the bustle of the dining hall and the peaceful solitude of the monk's walk.

"If 'twas the Lord who sent me, it must be because he could see just how hard the White Monks of St. Gabriel were on their clothes,'' she said, holding up the shredded hem and smiling at Francis.

"Sometimes I think we put too much on you, Bridget. How one slender girl can do all the work of caring for forty careless old men..."

"Forty dear souls," Bridget corrected. "Who first took care of *me* for many years, don't forget."

Francis looked doubtful. "It seems a burdensome life for a young woman."

Bridget gave the merry laugh that had so brightened the dark monastery halls and the lives of its inhabitants. "If it's a burden, then 'tis one of love," she said. "I'm fully content here."

Francis's worried expression smoothed. "If Brother Ebert tears his gown again, I'll see that he sews it himself," he promised. "He's so proud of his confounded bread slicer and I don't know how many times it's run amok." He turned to leave, muttering as he went, "I don't know what was wrong with pulling apart the bread hunk by hunk like we've always done."

Bridget smiled fondly at the round, retreating form. She'd told Francis the truth. She was content. It was true that sometimes, just before she drifted off to sleep, she'd have visions of a world beyond St. Gabriel. By morning the dreams would be gone.

She smoothed her fingers over the rough fabric of the torn habit and stared into the kitchen fire. She had no intention of looking for such a world. The only way she would glimpse it within these walls was if it would come to her.

Ranulf's initial thought was that another bird had shot out of the brush, this time knocking off the small leather helmet he was wearing. He hadn't brought his full armor to France. The wars were over and he had no desire for more fighting.

Almost immediately he realized that it had been no bird that had hit him, but an arrow. Before he could so much as reach for the sword in his saddle scabbard, they were on him. Four, at least, maybe more.

He flailed about with his arms, which were hard as an ironsmith's hammer. Even before the years of the Crusade, the three Brand brothers had honed their strength in friendly competition, always eager to match their mettle against their siblings.

With the sheer force of his blows, Ranulf knocked two of his assailants from their horses, but another, a big man dressed in a black breastplate and black metal wristlets, took their place. Ranulf's gloved fist hit the black metal, sending a shock all the way back up his arm. The man brushed Ranulf's arm away as though it were a noisome fly, then he turned in the saddle and lifted the weapon he held in his right hand.

The last thing Ranulf remembered was the sight of a wicked star mace and an arm encased in black wristlets descending toward his head, blotting out the bright Normandy sun.

"Brother Alois says we can't risk having you tend the man, Bridget." Francis's expression was worried.

"Nonsense. He's been out of his head, raving, for nigh on two days. The Holy Father himself could be nursing him and he'd not know the difference." Bridget finished stirring the mug of herbal tea at the edge of the hearth and rose to her feet. "Don't worry, Francis, if he starts to come around, I'll scurry back into the shadows like a little spider."

Francis's smile was sympathetic. "You know that if anyone outside learned of your presence here, you'd not be allowed to stay with us."

"Aye, I'm well aware of it."

Bridget scooted around the bulky monk, making sure not to spill the tea. It was one of the rare days when the brothers' overprotective ways irritated her. She was sure her dissatisfaction had something to do with the young man who lay unconscious in the monks' sleeping quarters. She'd caught a glimpse of him when Brother Ebert and Brother Alois had first brought him in the previous day. They'd found him on the road on their way back from market day in Beauville.

"I'll go with you," Francis said, giving a little puff as he lifted himself from the kitchen bench.

"You'll not," Bridget replied firmly. "I can't tend the patient and my stew at the same time. Just sit there and give it a stir every now and then."

Francis looked doubtfully from the young woman to the bubbling kettle and back. "You won't...*touch* the man, will you?"

Bridget rolled her eyes. "'Twould be quite a feat to feed tea to a senseless man without touching him, don't you think?"

"I should go with you."

"You should mind the stew. I'll be back in a few minutes, and if those carrots are scorched to the bottom of the pot, I'm sending you to dig me some new ones."

With a little sigh of relief, she ducked out the low door of the wooden kitchen and walked across the yard to the low brick dormitory that housed the Cistercian monks of St. Gabriel. When she was a child, growing up within the walls of the abbey, this building had been forbidden to her, but the practicality of her efficient housekeeping and sense of order had long since overcome the monks' scruples about allowing her access to their bedchambers.

Nowadays she had the run of the entire abbey, and used both smiles and a firm hand to keep it operating with the precision of the water timepiece Brother Ebert had invented. She rarely had problems, since the monks adored her, but some of them were a little...*absentminded* was the kind word, she decided. So she made it part of her routine to give gentle reminders when it was time to feed the animals, tend the vegetables, remove the week's baking from the oven, pour the tallow into molds before it boiled entirely away....

She smiled as she walked inside the building into the largest sleeping room. Around the walls were sixteen beds, lined up perfectly and with covers folded and neatly stacked on top of each cot. Before she'd taken charge, the monks had never had individual beds. The neatness had taken some doing, but it had now become routine.

Remembering her mission, she walked quickly through the other two sleeping rooms to the far end of the building where two individual chambers held single cots reserved for brothers who were ill. Bridget had often tended to sick brothers in the past, though she knew that her charges were never entirely comfortable with her ministrations.

They'd placed the stranger in the rear chamber.

A single candle flickered on the stand next to his bed and more light filtered in from the small window at the far end of the room. For a moment, she stood in the doorway, studying him.

There had not been a new novice to enter the order at St. Gabriel in Bridget's lifetime, which meant that the youngest of the brothers who had raised her was old enough to be her father. When the odd visitor had entered the abbey walls, the monks had always bustled her away into hiding before she could be seen. This was the first time, Bridget realized, that she had ever been in the same room with someone *young.* The man lying so still on the cot in front of her looked to be not much older than she herself.

His head was swathed in bandages and his face was stark white where it was not streaked with crusted blood. His eyes were closed, and appeared sunken in his skull. All in all, he was a rather gruesome sight, she decided, but fascinating for all that.

Brother Ebert and Brother Alois had found the man stripped of anything that could possibly identify him. He'd been beaten and left for dead. Such things happened in the outside world, Bridget knew, which was just one more reason why she should be content with her tranquil life behind the walls.

The tea was growing cold in her hands. She

walked over to the bed and placed the mug on the candle stand. The stranger lay so still that for a moment she wondered if he was breathing. Then her eyes moved to his chest and she saw an almost imperceptible rise and fall. He wore a thin undertunic that was stiff with dried blood. The sight of it, along with his bloody and battered face, gave her a shiver. Before anything else, the man could stand a good cleaning.

With sudden resolve, she spun around and marched back out through the monks' chambers, across the yard and into the kitchen. A dozing Francis bolted upright in his seat.

"I've stirred it well, lass," he said, the words thick.

Bridget paid him little attention. "Pray continue to do so, Francis. The fate of tonight's supper is in your hands."

Then she took an iron pot lifter from the wall and retrieved a kettle from the back of the fire.

Francis leaned forward. "What are you doing?"

"I need hot water."

"For more tea?"

"Nay. I mean to bathe the man."

Francis's jaw dropped. "*Bathe* him?"

"Aye. He's filthy with blood and dirt. How can we tend his wounds if we can't even see them?"

"'Tis an outrageous plan, Bridget. For one thing,

a bathing could finish what the brigands started.
And for another…why, child, you can't seriously
be thinking of…'' He stopped and clasped his
hands together under the long sleeves of his habit.

Bridget spoke briskly as she wrapped her skirt
around the handle of the kettle and started out of
the room. ''Just forget that I ever told you about it,
Francis. And mind the carrots,'' she called over her
shoulder.

She was still smiling when she reached the sick-
room. She couldn't remember ever seeing quite the
same look of consternation on Brother Francis's
kind face. It was wicked of her to enjoy it, but
she'd had so little chance to do anything out of the
ordinary, much less shocking, in her life here. This
was an adventure, even if it only meant cleaning
up a stranger who, from the look of him, was des-
tined for the tiny graveyard behind the chapel.

The room's candle had burned out in a puddle
of tallow, but the late afternoon sun slanted through
the tiny window, providing plenty of light. After a
moment of hesitation, Bridget set her shoulders and
walked over to the cot. She put the kettle on the
floor and sank to her knees beside it, bringing her
face only inches away from the sleeping man.

This close, she could see the stubble of whiskers
along his square jaw. She had a sudden urge to
know what they felt like, and, realizing that there

was nothing to prevent her from doing so, she reached out a gentle finger and stroked his chin. The harsh prickle surprised her. She pulled back as though burned, then touched him once again, more slowly.

His sunken eyes were rimmed with thick black lashes. Tendrils of hair escaping from his head dressing were black as well. What color were his eyes? she wondered.

Giving herself a little shake, she took one of the rags she'd brought along, soaked it in the hot water and began to wash him. The dried blood was two days old, and she had to rub to remove it. Her patient moaned and shifted restlessly on the cot, but did not awaken.

She removed his bandage to reveal an open, oozing gash along the side of his head. After supper she'd return with one of her herb poultices, but for the moment, she wrapped him back up in a new dressing. She finished washing his face, then his neck. Clean of the dirt and blood, his countenance was undeniably handsome, in spite of the pallor.

She reached the collar of his tunic and stopped, uncertain. It should come off, she decided. Now that his face was clean, the blood-soaked garment looked horrific. She threw the rag into the water and rose to her feet. The most sensible thing to do would be to leave the disrobing to the brothers. She had no doubt she was strong enough for the task—her days of hard work had made her stronger than many of the monks. But she had some doubt about the *propriety* of such an action.

She stood watching the patient for a long time, hesitating. He'd settled back into his deathlike stupor. In truth, she told herself, 'twas no different than cleaning up the bloody calf one of the milk cows had birthed last week. Taking a deep breath, she pulled the blanket from the inert man and threw it to the floor. Beneath the waist-length tunic, he wore woolen hose. Bridget gave a little gasp. She'd seen paintings in her books, but the only men she'd seen in person had been the monks, clad in their billowy robes. This man's legs bulged with sinewy strength. Between his legs were bulges of another sort.

At the pit of her stomach was a curious stirring.

She should definitely call the monks, she thought, even as she began to lift the man and strip the bloody tunic from his back. His naked chest was as hard and powerful as his thighs. Bridget swallowed, her mouth gone suddenly dry.

Without taking her eyes from the man's body, she leaned over to rinse the bloody rag in the cooling water. She was staring, she knew, but who was there to see? Then, with an impish grin at her own boldness, she proceeded to give the mysterious stranger a thorough washing from chest to…toe.

Ranulf couldn't understand why it was taking so long to cross the Channel. And why had they stuffed him into a barrel for the crossing so that he couldn't look out at the sea and sky? He tried to lift a fist to pound on the lid and demand release, but, to his amazement, his arm wouldn't move. Nothing would, for that matter.

Nothing was moving except the barrel, which made its regular up-and-down swoop with every new wave. Ranulf wanted to be sick, but even his stomach wouldn't move. Nor his mouth. His eyes wouldn't open, either. What had happened to him? he wondered in sudden panic.

The barrel surged again with the wave—up, up, then holding for an endless moment, then *down*. The movement sent a shaft of pain stabbing through his head. Jesu. What was wrong?

As the pain splintered light into his brain, the top of the barrel lifted and a beautiful, golden-haired woman peered in at him, smiling. He tried to call to her, but his throat closed around the words.

Darkness swirled, then she was there again—the golden angel. He made another desperate attempt to speak, but all he could produce was a moan of pain. His groan echoed off the sides of the barrel.

As the sound grew louder and louder, the angel slammed the lid of the barrel shut on top of him, and everything went black.

Brother Alois, acting abbot of St. Gabriel, seemed to assume that it had been Brother Francis who had bathed the wounded man and dressed him in one of the monks' own habits. Neither Bridget nor Francis bothered to correct him. But after her intimate session with the stranger the previous evening, Bridget had decided to let the monks take over the nursing. She'd spent one of her restless nights with visions of outside the walls. She dreamed that she'd accompanied the monks to market all the way to Rouen, walking freely beside them along the road, and that everyone they passed on the way looked like the handsome stranger lying in the monks' quarters.

She woke up resolving to stay away from the visitor, and kept her resolve throughout the day until evening when Francis came to request her help. "You mentioned one of your poultices, child, and I think it might help, for the poor lad has surely got the blood poisons."

She'd finished cleaning up from dinner and the monk had caught her leaving the kitchen, ready to retire to her little home next door to it. Long ago, the small brick building had been a brewery, and the faint, yeasty smell of ale still clung stubbornly to the masonry walls. But Bridget had lived there these past ten years or more, ever since the monks decided that she needed a place of her own with a sturdy door and proper latch.

It was not that they thought any member of their order capable of the unimaginable sin that those precautions suggested. But, Brother Alois had cautioned gravely, none of them had thought Bridget's father capable of such a transgression, either.

Bridget looked remorseful. "I'd meant to put a poultice on last night, but then I...I was distracted, I fear."

"Will you do it yet tonight or wait until the morrow?"

"It'd best be soon. I'll just prepare the paste and go on over to him."

Brother Francis looked up at the darkening sky. "I'll wait and go back with you."

"Nay, brother. You've been up tending him since well before dawn. Go on to your bed. It won't take me but a few minutes to see to him, then I'll be safely back to my house."

After a moment's more convincing, Francis turned to leave, and Bridget went back into the kitchen to prepare one of her medicinal poultices of marjoram and feverfew.

Bridget had begun to study the healing arts years

ago after the death of one of her favorite monks from a relatively minor injury. She'd spent nearly a month closeted in the monastery library, and then had persuaded Brothers Ebert and Alois to purchase herbs on one of their market forays. Since then, she raised the plants in her own garden, and the health of the monks of St. Gabriel had flourished accordingly.

It was dark by the time she made her way over to the monks' quarters. As she approached the building, she felt an odd excitement at seeing the stranger again. She slipped through the tiny back door that admitted her directly into the hall next to the wounded man's chamber.

After Francis's sober report, she was surprised at first to see that the patient looked better than he had the previous evening. But as she approached the bed, she saw that the improved appearance was due to a heightened color that was the ominous foreshadowing of seizures and death. She'd seen it before when wounds had become poisoned.

The gravity of the man's condition banished all other thoughts from her head, and she barely glanced at the lean body she had washed with such avid curiosity the previous day. She sat beside him on the narrow cot and removed the head bandages.

As before, he groaned at her touch, but she steeled herself to ignore the sound, and applied the poultice, pressing gently to be sure that the healing herbs would reach every part of the wound.

Under her fingers his scalp was burning. The man meant nothing to her. Indeed, if he recovered, his presence at the abbey could prove to be dangerous to her very existence. But she found herself offering up a quick prayer to St. Bridget. It seemed too cruel that death would take someone so young and so strong.

He moaned again as she rewound the bandage tightly to hold the herbs in place. "You must fight, Sir Stranger," she whispered. "Summon to battle the healing powers of your inner soul."

At her words, the wounded man stirred, then opened startling blue eyes and looked directly at her.

Chapter Two

Bridget gasped and pulled backward, letting the bandage slip from her hands. Her first thought was to flee, but as the head dressing started to unravel, causing the poultice to slip, she realized that she would have to finish the job she'd come to do and worry about the consequences later.

He watched her with unblinking eyes. "Are you awake, then?" she asked, hesitating.

He didn't answer. Perhaps the head wound had struck him dumb, she thought. Or perhaps he spoke no French. She repeated the question in Latin, with the same result.

As quickly as she could, she finished tying up the bandage, though it was unnerving to work on his head with his eyes open and staring. Even in the dim candlelight, their blue was intense.

"Do you understand me, sir?" she asked.

There was no movement of his dry lips.

Bridget sat for a moment. How ironic, she thought. These were the first words she had ever addressed to someone from outside the abbey, and they appeared to have no more impact than a milk-weed hitting a pond. She shivered. Perhaps she'd been born as some kind of otherworldly sprite, des-tined to live within the monastery walls and be seen and heard only by the monks. She'd read of faeries, but she'd never before believed herself to be one.

Could he see her? she wondered. She waved a hand in front of the man's eyes and was rewarded with a blink. She was, at least, not invisible.

Of course, it was just as well that he couldn't understand her, but she couldn't hold back a sense of disappointment. She was curious to know more about their visitor. Where had he come from? What had happened to him? She rose to her feet with a sigh. Now that he appeared to be regaining his senses, she would not be able to come here again.

"Angel," he said, the word an almost unrecog-nizable whisper.

Bridget stopped and turned back to the bed. She'd finished her nursing and, if the man was talk-ing, she should leave immediately. Instead, she walked back over to the cot and sank to her knees beside it. "Can you hear me?" she asked him.

"Bandits," he rasped.

"Aye, you were set upon, evidently, and they've given you a nasty gash, but we're taking care of you. I've treated you with some herbs."

Beads of sweat stood out above his lips. He appeared to try to swallow, then said, "Thirsty."

Bridget picked up a mug of tea that had been left on the floor and brought it to his lips. When it was apparent that he couldn't lift his head, she slipped an arm behind his neck and lifted him against her chest so that she could help him drink.

"Not too much," she cautioned.

He took another swallow, then sank back heavily against her arm. "Thank you, my angel."

Bridget smiled. "I'm no angel, just a maid." Her sudden fancy about being other than human had disappeared with this very human contact. The man could obviously see her and talk to her, and she to him. It was exhilarating.

There was an almost imperceptible shake of his head. "Angel," he insisted, then he clutched her arm with surprisingly strong fingers and said, "Help me."

His action startled her, but she answered, "Fear not, you're in safe hands now, good sir. No one will hurt you here."

"Help...find...Dragon," he said. His eyes had gone a little wild, and a dangerous flush had come over his face.

He was looking for a dragon? Is that what he had said? Bridget bit her lips. She'd read about dragons, but she'd formed the opinion that such a creature may not truly exist. "You must rest and get well. Let the monks tend your wounds until you heal."

"Diana," he groaned.

Bridget was confused. Perhaps it was a woman he was looking for, not a dragon. But in any event, he didn't have the strength to lift his head, much less go on a search. And this agitation could not be helping his cure. Perhaps she should brew him one of the sleeping teas she sometimes made for Brother Alois. "Can you not rest quiet?" she asked him. "'Tis the best thing for you now."

Bridget couldn't take her eyes from his striking features, which were full of anguish. He was so different from the monks. It wasn't just his youth— there was a raw strength about him that she'd never seen among the peaceful brothers at St. Gabriel.

Suddenly the hand that held her sleeve pulled her toward him. Startled, she fell against his chest. His arm came around her and, before she could react, his mouth touched hers. "I'll find him, Diana," he whispered.

Bridget jumped backward, one hand flying to her lips. She opened her mouth to give an indignant protest, but stopped as she saw that the patient had slumped back on the cot, his eyes closed and his mouth sagging.

She gave his shoulder a tentative shake, but he didn't respond. Her hands were shaking. She sat a moment, regaining her composure. He'd been out of his head, she assured herself. He'd obviously mistaken her for this woman, Diana. It had meant nothing.

But, nevertheless…she walked slowly from the tiny chamber and slipped out the back door into the cool night. The man had been delirious. He was a stranger, possibly even a malefactor. But nevertheless, she'd just had her first kiss.

"You were out of your head, my son. The mind plays tricks." Brother Francis's voice wavered slightly at the unaccustomed need for deceit.

"No, I swear, Brother. There was a woman in this room last night." Ranulf struggled to sit up, and looked around the tiny cell. The idea was preposterous. The monk had explained that he was inside a monastery, being cared for by the brotherhood. Yet his visions of the lovely midnight angel had seemed so real.

His head swam with pain and he lay back against the hard straw pad. "I could have sworn she was real," he said.

Francis smiled. "Mayhap 'twas a vision sent by

the Lord to guide you through your extremity. None of us thought that you would survive such a wound.'' He gestured to Ranulf's bound head.

The waves of pain were receding. ''I have to survive. I'm on a mission, and my family is depending on me to accomplish it.''

His family and others, as well. The image of Diana as he had last seen her, eyes flooded with tears, flashed through his head. He'd loved her as long as he could remember, but Diana's heart had always belonged to Dragon. And Ranulf was determined to bring him back to her.

''From the looks of you, young man, it appears that your mission is a perilous one.''

''Nay, no one knows me here. I believe the brigands set on me by chance.''

''They were robbers, then?''

''What else?'' Ranulf hesitated, trying to remember the scene. It seemed far away and unclear. He continued slowly, ''Though I believe they were too well mounted and outfitted to be common thieves. The man who struck me wore armor as fine as any I've seen.''

Francis gave a little shudder. ''There are still outlaw knights in this land. 'Tis a sad remnant of the holy effort to free the blessed sites of Christendom from the heathen.''

His attempt to recollect the incident on the road

was making Ranulf feel sick. His earlier visions of the golden-haired angel were much more pleasant, but although they'd seemed as real as the feel of the mattress straw prickling his neck, they had evidently been conjured up by his delirium. "So no woman has been tending me?" he asked with a little sigh.

The monk seemed to scrunch up his face. Then he made a quick sign of the cross and said loudly, "No. There's no woman at St. Gabriel Abbey."

It was just as well, Ranulf mused as the round little monk stood and bustled out of the room. In his dream, Ranulf remembered kissing her—his angel-vision. He'd been confused for a moment, thinking that he was with Diana again, taking his leave, promising her to find Dragon. Ranulf closed his eyes, remembering. His angel may have been a phantom, but the petal-soft touch of her lips still lingered on his mouth.

Most of the buildings at St. Gabriel were made of fieldstone, with roofs neatly thatched by the brothers' own hands. They formed a tidy quadrangle broken on one end by the graveyard that stood next to the monastery church. Isolated as it was in the wooded hills nearly two hours' walk from Beauville, the closest town, the church claimed no parishioners other than the brothers themselves, which suited them fine. That meant that they didn't have to deal with a procession of priests sent by the local bishop to meddle in their routine.

It also meant that few visitors came to explore the abbey grounds and take note of the odd building nestled in the woods about a quarter of a mile to the west of the church. The monks called the building the work shed, though it was far larger than any structure that would normally fit that term. It was as tall as the bell tower of the church, and, other than the barn, which housed the abbey's two mules, three milk cows and assorted other animals, it was the only building at St. Gabriel made entirely of wood.

Bridget avoided the work shed whenever possible. It was where the monks usually carried out their tinkerings, which was what the monks affectionately called their inventing efforts. One never knew what variety of odor or sound would be emanating from the ramshackle structure.

But when Francis failed to bring her a report on the progress of the patient, her curiosity made her seek the monk out at his afternoon labors.

Francis and Ebert had been spending an inordinate amount of time at the shed for the past fortnight. They'd traded their duties in the gardens with other monks so that they could continue work on their latest creation, which was a refinement of the water clock Ebert had invented.

She'd be the first to admit that the monks' ingenuity had made life easier at the monastery. She now had a spit that turned the meat automatically, driven by a device in the wall of the fireplace that turned with the heat of the fire. Of course, before the scheme had been perfected, she'd seen the ruin of at least half a dozen perfectly good roasts.

Bridget shook her head as she approached the building and was greeted with a barrage of loud bangs. She opened one of the huge wooden double doors and peered inside. Ebert was bent over his clock, a contraption consisting of small cups fastened around the edges of a wheel. Ebert was tall and thin. Even stooped over, his head rose above Brother Francis.

As Bridget entered, the clanging from the far end of the shed stopped. It had come from near the monks' special pride, a large furnace they had dubbed a blast fire because of the peculiar roar of the air through it and the force of the heat it generated.

Sometimes Bridget found herself drawn into the monks' plans, in spite of a resolve to stay detached, but today she had other things on her mind. She walked directly over to Francis and asked, "How is the patient? Has the poultice helped his wound?"

Francis's smile looked a little nervous. "It may have helped too well, child. He's regained his senses and had questions this morning about being nursed by a woman. A golden angel, he called you."

Bridget grinned. "I've always tried to tell you that I'm much holier than you give me credit for."

"'Tis not a cause for mirth, Bridget. It could have been disastrous, but I think I've convinced him that you were but a fever dream."

Bridget's grin faded. A fever dream. That was all she could ever be to anyone from outside of these walls. "If the fever's broken, he should have a new poultice," she said.

Ebert had straightened up to his full height and towered over both his fellow monk and Bridget. "Francis is right, Bridget. You must not be seen by the stranger again."

"Make up the poultice and I'll take it to him," Francis added.

Bridget felt an unaccustomed prickle of resentment. She had thought of little else but the wounded stranger all day long, and it seemed unfair that now that he had regained his senses she must hide herself away. "I should see the progress of the wound myself," she argued. "It will tell me what herbs to add to his cure."

Both monks regarded her gravely, shaking their

heads. "There's no way for you to see him, child," Francis said gently. "I'll give you a fair report."

Bridget bit her lip. The monks at the far end of the shed were watching the conversation. Sometimes it was difficult to tell the brothers apart at a distance in their identical habits, but she could somehow always recognize Brother Cyril. He was not plump like Francis, nor tall like Ebert, but there was just something about him, the way he moved, his energy and determination. Whereas most of the order were relaxed and happy, Cyril always seemed to be moving impatiently from one task to another. Bridget suspected that much less work would get done at the abbey without Brother Cyril's pushing.

Cyril and two other monks were working around the big furnace, but Bridget knew that including them in the debate would not help her cause. The monks were united in trying to protect her from the outside world.

"Is he of right mind?" she asked Francis. "Has he told you about himself?"

"Aye, he tells me his name is Ranulf."

"'Tis a Saxon name."

"Aye. He's English."

Bridget hid a little shiver of excitement. The man was not only from outside the walls of the abbey, he was from outside of Normandy itself. He had traveled the world, crossed the water. She had a fierce desire to talk with him. An hour or two in his company would no doubt teach her more than a month in the abbey library. It was impossible, of course. But at least she could *see* the man again.

"I'd like to check the wound myself," she said. "I'll wait until he's in a sound sleep tonight, then I'll just slip in and change the dressing. If I'm gentle, he shouldn't wake."

"'Tis a foolish risk to run for the sake of a stranger," Ebert observed.

"The stranger is nonetheless one of God's children, is he not, Brother Francis?" She appealed to the monk she knew to have the least resistance to her pleadings.

"Aye, but..."

"And therefore deserves no less care than the worthiest of saints. Is that not in the Rule?"

Though every waking minute of the Cistercian life was supposedly ordered by the sacred set of laws called the Rule, none of the monks of St. Gabriel were too well versed on exactly what the holy proclamation contained. Francis and Ebert exchanged a bewildered look, and Bridget seized her advantage.

"'Tis so, exactly," she exclaimed. "I've read it myself, and as a dutiful, if unofficial, daughter of this abbey, it's my place to abide by its teachings. I'll go to the stranger tonight while he's in a sound sleep. If he wakes up, he'll think it's his angel come to see him once again.''

"Child, we cannot—" Francis began.

"It's settled, then," Bridget interrupted, and before he could continue his argument, she spun around and skipped lightly out of the building.

Henri LeClerc, Baron of Darmaux and Mordin Castles, sat in his high-ceilinged receiving chamber at Darmaux and glared at the man in front of him as if he were some kind of bug that had crawled out from one of the cracks in the drafty stone wall.

"I didn't tell you to kill the man, Guise," he said. "I told you to find out why he was asking directions to St. Gabriel."

Charles Guise, sheriff of Beauville, did not flinch at the baron's scathing tones. "You were right, milord. The man was obviously a fighter. He put up more resistance than we had anticipated and I thought it best to get rid of him at once."

"You thought?" LeClerc stood and walked toward the sheriff until his odd violet eyes were only inches from Guise's. "You're not in my service to *think,* Guise. Now we have no idea what this English knight was doing here or how much he knew about the abbey."

The sheriff met LeClerc's gaze. "As I said, he

was a warrior. We may not have been able to take him alive.''

"Five of you? Against an unarmed knight? Do I have nothing but mewling babes working for me?''

Spit from the baron's vehement words flew into Guise's face, but the sheriff appeared to take no notice. "I'm sorry milord is displeased," he said.

LeClerc made a sound of exasperation and stalked back to his chair, sitting down heavily. "We should probably talk to our holy friend at the abbey to find out if he knows why the man was headed there.''

"It's some time before our monthly meeting, and we've agreed not to approach him on the abbey grounds.''

"I don't care how you manage it, just talk to him.''

"As you wish, milord.''

"What have you done with the body?''

For the first time, Guise looked uncomfortable. "It seems to have been...misplaced, milord.''

LeClerc's eyes narrowed into two violet slits. "Misplaced," he repeated slowly.

"Aye. After the skirmish, we rode away and by the time I had reconsidered the matter and sent some men back to dispose of him, the body was gone.''

All the fury had disappeared from the baron's tone as he said in silky tones, "Which means, my dear sheriff, that you aren't even sure that the man is dead."

"Oh, he's dead, all right. I can't imagine a head hard enough to survive the blow I gave him."

In the same deceptively soft voice, the baron continued, "I want this man found, Guise. Dead or alive."

"Aye, milord," the sheriff acknowledged with a bow.

"I suggest it be soon."

Guise's palms began to sweat. "Aye, milord," he said again. Then the baron waved him out of the room.

It had been easier to daydream about another visit to the sick man than it was to carry it out, Bridget realized as she stood in the little hall outside Ranulf's cell. What if he wasn't asleep? What if he awoke and this time realized that she was no holy creature but a flesh-and-blood woman?

What if he mistook her for the unknown Diana once again and tried to repeat his kiss? The thought sent a rush of blood to her cheeks.

With the warm poultice cooling in her hands, she took a deep breath and stepped into the dark room. Her candle flickered a dim light over to the bed.

Bridget gave a small sigh of relief as she saw that not only was the patient breathing in deep sleep, he was flushed with the night fever. Her ministrations could again be explained away in the morning as a dream.

She sat next to him on the bed. In spite of the fever, he looked better. The sunken shadows around his eyes were gone. She'd read that the Saxons were a fierce people. She'd wager this man could be fierce enough if pressed. She could read his strength in the broad line of his jaw and the power of his shoulders. Her gaze drifted to his full mouth. His lips on hers had not been fierce at all. They'd been tender and warm.

She straightened her shoulders. She had no business thinking about that kiss. Biting her own lip against the memory, she briskly began unwinding the bandage around his head. He moaned and half opened his eyes.

"Shh," she whispered. "It's all right. I'm here to help you get better."

"Angel," he rasped.

"Aye, 'tis your angel come to tend you once again. Close your eyes and sleep if you can."

But his eyes opened wider. "You're not Diana," he said.

He'd got that much straight, at least. "Is Diana your wife?" she asked.

With obvious difficulty, he shook his head and whispered, "She's to be…Dragon's wife."

"Nay, I'm not Diana. And there are no dragons here, sir, so you need have no fear. You're safe inside the abbey and we're going to see that you recover."

"Angel," he said again.

"I'll be your angel, if you like," she said. She pressed the poultice in place and made quick work of binding him up. He winced once but stayed still. When she had finished, she sat back and smiled at him. "It's much better, though the fever rages yet."

He reached up and grabbed her hand. "Who are you?" he asked.

The sudden clarity in his blue eyes unnerved her. "I thought we'd settled that," she said. "Didn't you say that I was your angel?"

His gaze moved slowly from her face to the place where her plain linen gown framed the soft skin of her neck and chest.

"Aye," he answered slowly, his voice growing stronger with each word, "but I was mistaken. If heaven had angels such as you to offer, my beauty, men would be falling on their swords in droves just to reach there."

All at once Bridget felt as if she were the one with a fever. Her cheeks flamed.

"There's the proof of it," Ranulf continued, gesturing weakly toward her face. "Angels can't blush."

The remark was so absurd that Bridget couldn't help a tiny laugh. "How do you know that, sir? I don't recall any such prohibition in the scriptures."

"They're holy creatures. They don't suffer from such human frailties as embarrassment or—" he stopped to study her, his eyes growing even more intense "—or *shyness*. Which is it that tints those fair cheeks so prettily?"

These were not the ravings of a delirious man, Bridget realized, in spite of his fever flush. This man was as sane as she and totally aware of her presence. She stood in alarm, the discarded bandage falling heedlessly to the floor. "I pray you, sir, close your eyes and sleep. On the morn you will remember that an angel tended you this night, and if you remember anything else about our encounter, I would ask you to put it out of your mind."

He reached for her hand. "Don't go, please. Be my angel, then, and I won't question you further, I promise. Just sit by me awhile longer and let me look at you."

His grasp was weak, and she could have easily slipped her hand loose, but instead she let him pull her gently back down to the bed. "I must go," she whispered. "You need rest."

For the first time, she saw him grin, a boyish, engaging smile that made the breath catch in her throat. "Ah, fair maid, they say to look upon beauty can be a more powerful cure than any herbalist's powder."

Once again Bridget's face flamed at the unaccustomed comment on her appearance. Her discomfiture made her answer sharply. "Who says such nonsense?"

"My grandmother Ellen, for one. And she's been healing the good folk of Lyonsbridge for three score years."

Each moment she continued talking to him compounded her risk, but her curiosity prickled. "Lyonsbridge? 'Tis your home?"

"Aye. It's in England, but my grandmother is Norman. She grew up here in Normandy."

Bridget tried to picture this Norman woman. What would it be like to travel to a strange land, to make a home there and raise a family? "Is your grandmother a healer?" she asked.

The man hesitated a moment, then said, "She tends her people as the lady of the estate."

Bridget's eyes widened. So this man who lay abandoned and helpless in their abbey was not an itinerant wanderer, but the grandson of a lord. That meant that there would no doubt be inquiries. If she and the monks didn't get him well and send him on his way soon, people might come to St. Gabriel looking for him.

She pulled her hand away from his and stood. "You've talked too long, milord," she said stiffly. "I must insist that you sleep."

"I'm no lord, angel. My name is Ranulf Brand. And since we've established that you're not one of the heavenly host, I'd like to know your name, as well."

Bridget shook her head. She could not tell this man her name. Outside these walls she had no name; she didn't exist.

"Won't you tell me?" he coaxed.

She shook her head again, more vigorously, then turned and fled the room.

Chapter Three

Like a moth drawn to the brightness of the fire, Bridget found herself obsessed with a dangerous desire to see the stranger again. She wanted to ask him all about his home across the water—this Lyonsbridge. She could only begin to imagine all that he could tell her of life outside the walls. But the monks had guarded the secret of her presence all these years. She didn't dare expose it. She would *not* see the Englishman again, she told herself firmly as she mechanically performed the morning chores. She would not even venture near the monks' quarters until he was safely away from the abbey.

But she could not rid herself of the memory of his blue eyes and teasing smile. His words ran over and over through her mind. Her ears rang with the sound of his deep voice as he'd called her "angel."

At midday she gave up the idea of getting in a good day's work and wandered across the courtyard toward the church. Her conscience told her that she should spend the rest of the day on her knees begging the Lord's forgiveness for being ungrateful for the life she'd been given. But instead, she turned away from the church door and went to the attached building, which housed the abbey's collection of manuscripts. As usual, the library was empty.

It was a poor collection compared to the great monasteries in other parts of Europe, but it contained the expected religious texts, which were dusted by one of the monks each month and rarely, if ever, read. The brothers of St. Gabriel were more interested in the scientific volumes, and these they kept out in the work shed, where they would be readily accessible.

Bridget sometimes thought of the library as her own private sanctuary. She'd read every single book many times, but she returned most often to a special cupboard that contained volumes deemed unsuitable for perusal by the brotherhood. She'd been nearly fifteen years old before she'd dared look inside. Once she'd begun, however, the books had become her favorites. She read the tragic Greek myth of Orpheus who had traveled all the way to the underworld to find his lost Eurydice. She sighed

over the love poems of Ovid. But she was most
fascinated with the tales of the great English king,
Arthur, and his bold knights.

She took out the volume and began to read,
though she could as well have recited the words by
heart. Was Ranulf a knight? she wondered. They'd
found him stripped of all possessions, but if he was
from a noble family, surely he had come on horse-
back. He did have the strength of a warrior, she
thought, flushing as she remembered the night
she'd stripped away his bloody tunic.

Eagerly her eyes raced over the familiar words.
Lancelot had come from the continent to England
to join Arthur's fabled court. There he had found
love with beautiful Guinevere. Now this knight, *her*
knight, had come from England to the continent on
his own noble mission. Would he too find love?
Bridget smiled at her own fantasy.

The knight lying in the monks' quarters dressed
in one of their habits had nothing to do with the
legendary Lancelot. Nor would a poor girl raised
in a forgotten monastery have anything in common
with the fabled English queen.

"Bridget! Are you in here?"

Brother Francis's voice interrupted her dreaming.
Quickly she closed the wooden cover of the big
book and slid it back on the shelf. "Aye, I've been
studying," she said, jumping up from the stool and

going to meet the monk at the door before he could pay too much attention to the corner of the room that had been occupying her attention.

Francis's face was grave, and Bridget's first thought was of the patient. "Is he worse?" she asked in alarm. "Has the fever heightened?"

Francis shook his head. "Nay, he's better. That's the problem. He's on his feet, even, and swearing to Alois that he intends to search the monastery until he finds the lovely nurse who has cured him."

Bridget winced. "Didn't you tell him I was part of the delirium?"

"Aye, sweet mischief maker. But this time he's too sure of his own faculties. He'll not hear me." He gave her a reproving gaze. "I told you 'twould be foolish to go to him again."

Bridget tipped her head, considering. "Well then, you'll have to tell him that I was a maid from Beauville whom you brought here to tend him. Send him there to search for her."

"I'd have to tell a falsehood—" he began.

"Forgive me, Brother, but how many falsehoods have you told these many years to keep my presence a secret? One more will do nothing to alter the toll, I wager."

"I'll think on it," he said. "But for the moment, I'm to bring you to Alois."

Bridget groaned. Alois was the abbot of St. Gabriel. He had always seemed to Bridget to be a fair man but, unlike Francis, he had absolutely no sense of humor. She knew that his reprimand for her actions would be much more severe than Francis's gentle chiding.

"The stranger himself said that I may have saved his life," she told Francis.

"Aye, child. We all know that your medicines can work wonders, but 'tis the other that has raised Brother Alois's concern."

"The other?" Bridget asked.

Francis averted his eyes and stumbled over the words as he explained, "This man—the, um, patient—he's claiming that he *kissed* you."

As it turned out, Bridget had had to face not only Brother Alois, but also Brother Cyril, the abbey prior, and Brother Ebert. She might have expected Ebert, since he was the brother who, by common consent, had most to do with the outside world. It had been Ebert who had first found the wounded stranger on the road, and Ebert was the monk who most often rode to the city when the necessity arose for some item that the monks could not grow or create themselves. Most often this meant something for one of the monks' inventions.

The three awaited her arrival sitting side by side on the high trestle bench in the small sacristy at the back of the church. They wore identical habits, since Alois refused to distinguish himself from the others by wearing abbot's robes. Bridget knew she had nothing to fear from them, but at the moment they resembled three vultures perched on a log.

Francis stood next to her as she stopped in front of them.

"My child," Alois began. "You have been our charge these many years, and every one of us in this brotherhood has vowed to protect and care for you."

"I know, Brother, and I'm sorry if I've caused—"

Alois held up a hand. "'Tis no fault of yours, Bridget. The fault was ours for not realizing how difficult it would be to keep you from the world now that you've grown into a—" the abbot stumbled over the words "—into a mature woman."

Bridget had been called to account before for minor transgressions, but she sensed something different about this audience. She was used to gentle chiding, a softly reproving smile. Instead the expressions on the faces of her three accusers seemed to reflect something resembling fear.

"I'm sorry," she murmured.

Brother Ebert leaned forward. "Do you have something to tell us, Bridget? Did this man—this stranger—do anything—anything—"

He stopped. The words were beyond even the worldly Ebert.

Bridget felt a tug at her heart. What Alois had said was true. The brothers had cherished and protected her as if they had been her parents, but somewhere along the line it seemed almost as if she had become the mother and they the sons. She knew little of the world, but thanks to her readings, she probably had more sense than any of them about what could happen between a man and a maid. She could see that the monks were afraid for her, and that they had no earthly idea how to communicate either that fear or the love that inspired it.

She wished she could go to each one of them and give them an embrace, but that, of course, was forbidden by the Rule. Instead she tried to put her feelings into her smile. "You can stop worrying about me. Nothing passed between me and our visitor. Perhaps I should not have tended to him myself, but there's no help for that now."

Cyril was tapping a foot nervously on the crossbar of the bench. "She says nothing happened. What more do you want from the girl?" he asked impatiently. "Make her promise not to see him again, and let's be done with it."

Bridget rarely saw Cyril outside of the work shed, and she imagined he was anxious to return to whatever experiment he was currently conducting.

Ebert nodded agreement, but Alois looked uncertain. "As abbot, I must be sure."

Francis, who'd been standing next to Bridget, spoke for the first time. "The man was in a fever, brothers. He scarcely remembers what transpired, and soon he'll be gone. I don't think we need to take any further action."

With his three brother monks waiting for his word, Alois finally nodded agreement. "Do you promise, Bridget?" he asked.

Bridget nodded. "I'll stay well out of sight until he's gone."

Alois let out a long breath. "Very well, then. We'll speak of the matter no more." The three monks stood with noticeable sighs of relief, then filed silently out of the room.

Ranulf sat on the edge of the bed hoisting the heavy cloth belt in his hand. The thieves who had robbed him, if they had been thieves at all, had either been incredibly impatient or stupid. They'd taken his horse, his weapons, his outer clothes, even his boots, but they'd left him wearing a small fortune beneath his undertunic. And the plump little monk had just restored it to him untouched. For a man who'd been nearly beaten to death, Ranulf was amazingly lucky.

"How far is this town, Brother?" he asked Francis. "And what's the maid's name? I'd like to visit her home to thank her and compensate her for her service."

The monk's cheeks jiggled as he gave a vigorous shake of his head. "She'd not receive you, sir. Nay, 'tis best left alone. The only reward any of us wish is your return to good health. With the fever gone, it shouldn't be long before you regain your strength and can be about your business."

Ranulf was not ready to tell the monk that his business was to begin here at St. Gabriel. He wanted his strength back and his head totally clear before he began his inquiries about Edmund.

"I appreciate what you *all* have done for me, Brother," he said, "but I believe it was the maid's medicine that saved my life, and I don't intend to leave without showing my gratitude."

Francis sighed. "Beauville is a long ways from here, Sir Ranulf. You're not yet strong enough for the trip."

Ranulf's head still hurt, but his mind had regained its sharpness. Something in the monk's words confused him. "If she lives so far from here, how was it that she was tending me in the middle of the night?"

"You must be mistaken," Francis answered stiffly. "She comes at midday."

Ranulf glanced at the tiny window where a shaft of sunlight pierced the gloom of his cell. Had he been that muddled? he wondered. Or were day and night all one in this foreign land?

"She treated me by candlelight. I remember it distinctly."

"Ah, sir, you were in too sorry a state to remember anything distinctly. Now I think it's time for you to lie down and get some sleep, lest you fall back into the delirium you've just left."

Ranulf looked from the monk down to the money in his hand. "Shall I give this back to you for safekeeping?" he asked.

Francis laughed. "You need have no fear of thieves inside the walls of St. Gabriel. Your coin has no value to us here."

Ranulf shook his head in wonderment. He'd never met such men before. The monks who had tended him seemed to be uniformly content with their lot. They appeared to have none of the failings of ordinary men—greed, ambition, desire.

He dropped the heavy belt to the dirt floor beside his bed. "I'll just leave it here for now. But though your holy brotherhood may have no interest in my gold, I'll warrant my nurse would find good use for a few of these coins. I still intend to seek her out when I can mount a horse."

"Mules are the only mounts you'll find here at the abbey."

"Until I can mount a mule, then." Ranulf grinned. "I haven't been on one since I was a page, but I won't disdain the beast if it will take me to where I can outfit myself anew."

"They are steady creatures, I'm told, though I haven't been on one myself. I keep meaning to give it a try."

Ranulf bit back a laugh at the picture of the rotund little monk on top of a mule. "Perhaps we'll go seek the maid together—when I'm well enough."

"Perhaps," Francis said with a nervous smile. "Now, sleep. The sooner you regain your strength, the sooner you can be back on your journey."

Ranulf nodded and settled back on his cot. The monk seemed anxious to be rid of him, and even more anxious to avoid his questions about the beautiful woman who had come at least twice to his bedside. There was something odd about the monk's story of a village maid, and it *had* been night when she had visited him. He was sure of it. He didn't understand why they were being so evasive, but he was determined to find out. He was anxious to begin his inquiries about Dragon, but his brother had been missing for three years—the quest could wait another day or two while he solved the riddle of his mysterious angel healer.

* * *

It was good to feel the sunshine on his face, Ranulf thought, especially considering how close he'd come to never feeling anything ever again.

"So where is this magnificent mule you've promised me, Brother?" he asked Francis as they walked across the courtyard toward the barn.

The monk smiled. "Are you sure you're ready to try riding? Your wound is still fresh."

"Aye, but my brain is like to rot from the inside out if I don't get away from that cell for a while. I'll just give it a try, and see how it feels again to be up on a mount—*any* mount," he added with a rueful twist of his mouth. He'd brought Thunder, his big gray stallion, all the way across the Channel only to have him taken by his assailants. The loss hurt more than his head wound.

"At least our mules will give you no trouble. They're old and lazy. They had other names once, but for years now they've been called Tortoise and Snail."

Ranulf joined in the round monk's hearty laugh as they reached the open barn doors and went inside. The mules faced each other in stalls on opposite sides just inside the entryway.

"Which is which?" he asked.

Francis started to answer, then stopped as a scurrying sound caused both men to turn their heads toward the back door of the barn. Ranulf's eyes had not adjusted to the dim interior, but as he looked toward the patch of daylight coming through the small rear entry, he saw a slim shape dash around the edge of the door and disappear.

Francis cleared his throat loudly. "This is Tortoise," he said, taking Ranulf's shoulder and turning him toward the right-hand stall.

Ranulf twisted his head to look back toward the far door. He was almost sure that the figure he'd seen slipping through it had been a woman.

"Has my nurse come to visit from her town?" he asked Francis.

The monk shook his head. "Nay. She'll not return now that you're well."

"I thought I saw—" He nodded toward the rear of the barn.

"The stable boy? He comes to muck the stables every few days."

Ranulf frowned. "I thought you said the monks did all their own work here."

"Aye, except for—except for this, er, stable boy. He lives on a farm nearby, from a poor family, he needed the work...."

In Ranulf's experience, men who had taken holy vows were invariably honest, but once again he had the feeling that the congenial Francis was trying to deceive him. He'd caught only a glimpse of the figure in the barn, but he was now almost certain that it had been the young woman he was seeking.

He listened absentmindedly as Francis introduced him to the two mules, who, while not Thunder, were not the sorry creatures he'd feared. Either one would do to get him as far as a town where he could purchase a new mount and weapons.

He reeled with a wave of dizziness as he swung up onto the back of the one they called Snail, but soon recovered his balance. A short walk around the barn was all he needed to see that he was perfectly capable of riding once again, though he did tire quickly.

He'd give himself a day or two more to recover, he decided, handing the animal back over to Francis. In the meantime, he'd try to discover why the monk was lying to him about his beautiful midnight nurse.

Bridget raced around the back of the abbey buildings and darted inside the kitchen, breathing heavily. It had been a narrow escape. She'd promised to stay safely hidden while the stranger was still at St. Gabriel, but she'd come seconds away from running smack into him.

"How was I to know Francis would bring him wandering around the barn?" she asked aloud to the abbey cat who lay curled beside the fire. The tawny animal gave a delicate yawn and went back to its nap.

At first, Bridget had thought the man was another of the monks. He still wore the habit she'd dressed him in that first night. But it had taken only moments for her to realize her mistake. Even in the rough habit, you could see the visiting knight's broad shoulders and powerful arms. And the robe ended well above his ankles, since he was taller than every brother in the abbey, with the possible exception of Ebert.

Bridget lifted the stone jug from the table and poured herself a cup of ale. She was hot and irritated. She knew that the monks were right to keep her from the visitor, but she hated having to run away like a frightened rabbit.

"What would be the harm in a few minutes of conversation with the man?" she asked the cat, who raised its head again with an expression of annoyance. "He'll ride away soon and forget he ever saw me here. Would it be the end of the world or the end of St. Gabriel to have one person from the outside learn of my presence here?"

The cat's only answer was the continued stare of its big black eyes. It appeared to be waiting to see if there would be further interruptions of its mid-morning slumber. When Bridget remained silent, the big furry animal stretched out its front paws and lay back down to sleep.

The monks of St. Gabriel had a schedule of duty—kitchen, garden, repair, animals—that they rotated to give everyone a fair turn. Bridget had devised the system. Until she had taken charge, work had been performed haphazardly. She participated in much of the work herself, but caring for the animals was not among her assigned tasks. She did, however, make it a practice to check the barn daily to be sure that everything had been done properly.

Any lapses would not be due to laziness or lack of will. But more than once a monk who was engrossed in testing a new method for making gates open by themselves would forget that he had left a cow unmilked or the pigs with no feed.

The sudden arrival of Francis and Ranulf had prevented her from making her normal morning rounds. Missing a day would make little difference, but when she finished cleaning up after the evening meal, she decided to give the barn a quick walk-through before she retired to her little house.

The long spring twilight was fading as she opened the heavy barn doors. Patches of pink sky showed through two openings in the roof of the big building, but the interior was dimmer than during her usual visiting hours. She should have brought a lantern, she thought. A gust of wind through the doors at her back made her shiver.

The barn was quieter than in the daytime. Some of the animals had already nestled down for sleep. The two mules tossed their heads as she passed, but quickly lost interest when they saw that her hands were empty of the carrots she occasionally brought them.

She moved along the center aisle, her eyes skimming over the three cows, the coop full of chickens. Everything seemed in order, and the sky above her was growing darker by the moment.

Shrugging off a sense of unease, she turned to leave.

Suddenly a hand grasped her arm and an unmistakable deep voice said, "Good evening, angel."

Chapter Four

Bridget gasped and spun around to look up into blue eyes that were kindled with amusement.

"Do you come by night to nurse animals as you do wayward travelers?" he asked.

She opened her mouth to speak, but her throat felt clogged with hay dust from the stable floor. "I—I—" she stuttered.

His smile died as he saw the panic in her expression. "Calm yourself, angel. I didn't mean to alarm you. I've been looking for you these two days past in order to thank you for my cure." He pointed to his still-bandaged head. "I probably owe you my life."

"Nay, 'twas nothing. I must go." She twisted sideways to pull her arm from his grasp, but he held her firmly.

"I won't hurt you, mistress. I promise. Don't run away again."

Bridget's head was ringing with the dire warnings the brothers had given her over the years about what would befall them all if her presence became known. The dangerous game she had played with the stranger was no longer a game. It was obvious he was too well recovered to ever be convinced that seeing her had been another dream.

"You don't understand," she pleaded. "I beg you, let me go."

For another long moment, their eyes held, hers anguished, his puzzled. Then he released his hold on her arm. Without another word she pushed past him, ran out of the barn and into the darkening night.

Ranulf stood staring after her retreating form for several moments. One of his questions had been answered, at least. The maid was real. It was no wraith whose strong, slender arm he had held. The face that had looked up at him with such alarm was not that of an otherworldly creature, but of a flesh-and-blood woman with a sprinkle of freckles across her nose and a wild-rose blush painting her cheeks. The lips he'd once touched with his own in the throes of his fever had been full and red.

He realized with sudden shock that his brief encounter with the mysterious young woman had left him shaky with something akin to desire. Jesu. He'd never been a man to woo and love lightly. In fact, he'd scoffed at those of his fellow Crusaders who were desperate enough to seek out the women of the stews to ease their bodily needs.

He'd always preferred to turn his own thoughts to loftier channels. Though he'd never admitted it to anyone, he'd often used the vision of Dragon's promised bride, Diana, when the weariness of battle had made him long for more tender thoughts of women and home. Oddly enough, Diana's ethereal beauty suddenly seemed tame next to the memory of the woman he'd just confronted in the barn.

He looked around him. Night had fallen, and the animals had grown quiet. He could barely make out their forms in the darkness. He started walking slowly toward the doorway, his mind whirring with questions. Why had she fled? What was she afraid of? And why had Brother Francis lied about her?

He reached the courtyard and squinted to see across it in the dusk. There was no sign of his beautiful nurse. Across the square was the church with the small cemetery beyond. On his left were the monks' quarters and to the right a kitchen. The small brick building beyond that? Could she have gone there?

He continued walking to the middle of the square. The tiny building had no window, and there was no light showing from underneath the crack of the door. If his nurse was inside, she was sitting in the dark.

Ranulf sighed. He did not yet have enough strength to search the whole compound for her, especially at night. His lifesaver would remain a mystery for another night.

Francis had consulted with Brother Ebert and Abbot Alois.

"Bridget, it's simply too dangerous for you here right now," Alois told Bridget gently as she sat in stunned silence on his bed in the abbot's chamber. "The Marchands are kind people. They'll give you a good home. If anyone discovers you there, Mistress Marchand has agreed to introduce you as her niece, the daughter of a sister who has died."

"That would mean living with some deceit, Bridget," Ebert added. "But no more than we have all had to bear over the years. I'm sure God will forgive us since it has all been done in an effort to keep you safe."

Bridget shook her head and said firmly, "I won't go. What would you do without me here?"

Francis sat beside her on the abbot's narrow cot and, ignoring the conventions of his order, put an arm around her and drew her against his plump shoulder. "We shall have to manage, Bridget.

We're not totally helpless, you know. We did get on somehow before you came.''

''But the kitchens…the gardens…the work orders…'' Bridget could not believe what she was hearing. They were sending her away from the only home she'd ever known, all because she'd exchanged a few sentences with a stranger who would no doubt continue on his travels and never bother them again.

''We'll all miss you dreadfully, Bridget, and we'll try to keep the abbey from falling apart in your absence.'' There was a touch of amusement in Alois's voice.

''You may like it on the outside, Bridget,'' Ebert added. ''It's time you had a life of your own that involves more than caring for a bunch of old men.''

Bridget looked up at Francis, who still held her clutched to his side, then at the anxious faces of Alois and Ebert hovering over her. She was beginning to realize that, unlike times in the past when she'd been able to sweet-talk or bully the monks into seeing her side of things, this time they were not about to be swayed. ''I've never wanted any life but this,'' she said, her voice faltering. ''I'm happy here. Please don't send me away.''

Alois straightened up. ''It's already decided. Ebert will take you tomorrow before dawn. By the time our English visitor wakes up, you'll be gone.

Now you'd best get some sleep before your journey.''

Her momentary weakness past, Bridget slipped out of Francis's arm and stood, facing all three of them, her hands on her hips. "I won't go," she said again. "I'm sorry that I've worried you by speaking with the stranger, but he'll be soon gone, and I'm not going to let his visit disrupt the life of this entire abbey.''

Francis rose heavily to his feet. "I'm afraid the abbot is right, Bridget. It's the only way to protect you. What would people think if they knew you'd been raised among us?''

"I don't care what they think.''

"Ah, but you profess to care what becomes of this abbey," Alois said gravely. "And if it were known that we had kept you hidden here all these years, it could endanger our very existence.''

This was an argument Bridget had not considered. "Do you think the church would—''

"Holy orders have been disbanded for less grievous offenses," Alois interrupted.

She sat back down on the bed in stunned silence. Though she could hardly fathom the thought, it appeared that she might have no choice but to agree to the abbot's decision. She was going to be banished from her home and all the people she loved.

Struggling with rising tears, she said, "Promise

me that once the stranger leaves, you'll let me return.''

Francis gave a sad smile. ''Lass, you're about to
discover a whole new world that you've never before experienced. By the time the Englishman
leaves us, you may not want to return here.''

''I shall want to return here,'' she said fiercely.
''St. Gabriel is my home, and it always will be.''

The monks exchanged a sad glance, but none of
them tried to argue with her.

''So as soon as he leaves, you'll have me back?''
she asked again.

''We'll discuss the matter at that time,'' Alois
said stiffly.

And she had to be content with that.

Ranulf found Brother Francis leaving church after morning prayers.

''How's your head today?'' Francis greeted him.
It seemed to Ranulf that some of the monk's usual
enthusiasm was missing.

''Each day a little better,'' Ranulf replied. ''But
I've not sought you out to discuss my condition.
I've come for some answers.''

Francis looked around. A number of the monks
were leaving the church, making their way to their
morning tasks. He nodded his head toward the far
end of the courtyard. ''We'll talk over at the veg-

etable garden," he said. "It will be more private, and in any event, I'm on cook duty today."

Neither man spoke until they had crossed to the other side of the compound and reached the good-sized plot of land where the monks grew most of their produce. Francis picked up a basket from the edge of the tilled area and gestured with it toward Ranulf. "Did they ever set you to harvesting vegetables in that fancy estate of yours, lad?"

But Ranulf was not about to be distracted from his purpose. He ignored the monk's question and the offered basket, saying instead, "I saw her again last night, Brother Francis—the midnight nurse. Why did you lie to me about her?"

Francis hesitated, then set the basket back on the ground and turned to face the younger man. "May the Lord forgive me, son, but I had my reasons. I'll ask you to inquire no further about the maid."

"But why? Can't I at least have an explanation? This woman saved my life, remember."

"I'm sorry."

"You'll not give me her name? Nor tell me where I can find her?"

"I cannot."

Ranulf wondered at his own insistence in the face of Francis's obvious misery. He should forget the girl and put his mind on the business of finding his brother, but something compelled him to find out about her. His head was starting to throb again. He set his jaw and returned the monk's implacable gaze. "Then I'll make my own inquiries. I warrant someone in town will be able to tell me about her. There can't be too many young women of her description with the healing powers."

Francis winced, then he hiked the hem of his habit, knelt awkwardly at the side of the vegetable patch and reached once again for the basket. "You are a very stubborn young man," he said.

"Aye. So I've been told."

"She's no longer here," Francis said finally, beginning to pick beans off a tangled vine. At Ranulf's skeptical expression, he glanced up at him and continued, "I'm telling you the truth this time. She left this morning for Beauville. But you must believe me when I tell you that inquiries could put her very life in danger."

This was not what Ranulf had expected. He'd speculated about different reasons for the monk's reluctance to tell him about the girl, but this notion had not been among them. Looking around at the gentle green hills that surrounded the humble abbey, he asked, "What could threaten a young maid's life in this peaceful place?"

Francis continued his methodical picking. "Once again, I can't tell you. 'Tis a secret guarded over these many years. But I would beg you to put her out of your mind.''

Suddenly Ranulf's curiosity about the beautiful maid took on a whole new meaning. If the monk's words were true—if his mysterious nurse was truly in danger—then perhaps he'd been brought here to help her. He'd seen such miracles before on Crusade.

''I'd like to help her,'' he said.

His tone was so earnest that Francis put down the basket once again and dropped his head to his chest, lost in thought.

Sensing that the monk was weakening, Ranulf pressed his case. ''I'd do nothing to harm her, Brother. I swear it by the holy rood. And perhaps it would be in my power to help her.''

''I don't think there's anything you can do to help,'' Francis said slowly. ''But if you give your sacred word never to speak to anyone of the circumstances under which you met her, I'll tell you where she is. You may go to thank her and give her whatever reward you would like for the services she rendered you.''

Ranulf felt a peculiar elation that seemed out of proportion to the simple fact that he would have the opportunity to give a proper payment to a young woman who had tended him. ''Where is she?'' he asked eagerly.

Francis shook his head. "First, your word."

"That I'll not speak of her?"

"Aye."

It seemed a strange request, but Ranulf nodded. "Aye, you have my word."

Brother Francis looked into the basket. The bottom was scarcely covered. With a grunt, he pushed himself off the ground with both hands and stood. "The information will cost you," he said, dusting off his hands.

Ranulf nodded. "My money is still in my room. I'll fetch it—"

Francis broke him off with a slight smile. "I don't want your money, young man. The price will be that basket of beans." He stabbed toward the basket with his finger. "I'll expect it full to over-flowing. When you have gathered the fee, you'll find me in the kitchen."

As the monks had promised, Claudine and Philip Marchand were kind people, though they were both stooped with age. In some ways their frailty was comforting, for Bridget immediately set about putting their small thatched house to rights, cleaning and organizing and cooking a hearty meal, and for a time she could almost think that she was back at the abbey.

She and Ebert had left St. Gabriel before dawn,

plodding along on Snail and Tortoise. She'd been utterly aware that each step was taking her farther away from the only home she'd ever known, but the time on the road had given her a chance to think about the positive aspects of her adventure. She was going to see something of the world outside! Even if she never saw more than a peasants' home outside of humble Beauville, it was farther than she had ever journeyed before.

By the time they reached the Marchands' tiny cottage, she was able to say goodbye to Ebert with barely a quiver of emotion in her voice, asserting once again that she would be back at St. Gabriel as soon as the stranger had left.

Then she had turned to the embrace of old Mistress Marchand and felt a rush of warmth that evoked feelings from a time beyond her memories. She wondered fleetingly if she had once been held like this by another woman, tender and bosomy, but the idea seemed impossible. The only embraces she'd had in her life had been the rare ones the monks had given her while she was growing up. She now understood that each one of those gestures had been against the Rule, which meant she valued them all the more.

Philip Marchand had contented himself with a kindly pat on her shoulder as a welcome. Bridget soon discovered that the well-meaning man was

nearly deaf, and sometimes more than a little confused, but his wife watched over him with the fierce
love of a mother hawk to be sure that he came to
no harm.

"I'm afraid we'll be poor company for a pretty
young thing like yourself," Claudine told her as
they waved Brother Ebert down the road and turned
to go inside.

"Nay, 'tis kind of you to have me," Bridget assured her. Then after a few more pleasantries, she'd
begun to look around the cottage for tasks to per-
form—and she'd found them in abundance.

The activity made the first day away from home
go quickly, and, as Bridget lay down to sleep that
night in a small loft at the back of the house, she
decided that this interlude might not be so disagree-
able after all. The monks had chosen the Marchands because the older couple now had little contact with the rest of the community, and their home
was at some distance from the town. It was possible
that she would be able to go back to the abbey
before anyone else even knew of her presence here,
and in the meantime, the Marchands could benefit
from her help.

Of course it was tempting, now that she'd taken
this first step, to go out and explore the rest of
Beauville, but if she did that, more questions might
be raised. It was best to stay hidden, she decided,

as sleep slowly claimed her. Then soon she would be able to go home.

"I don't understand what any of this has to do with St. Gabriel, lad," Francis said as the two sat by the kitchen fire long after most of the monks had retired. Though Ranulf had already caught him in a lie, he was virtually certain the puzzlement in the monk's voice was genuine.

"I'm not sure, either, Brother. All I know is that the last word we heard from Edmund was a letter sent to his affianced bride. He told her he was heading toward an abbey of White Monks called St. Gabriel. This is the only such place we could locate."

"Aye, I know of none other."

"But you don't have any idea why my brother would have wanted to come here?"

"I don't know why anyone would want to come here, son. Why, it's been nigh on twenty years now since our own bishop has paid us a call."

Ranulf stared into the dying embers of the fire. "Mayhap he meant that he was coming to your town."

"Beauville? 'Tis as unlikely a choice as the abbey itself. Beauville's a sleepy place known for the fine size of its vegetables at the weekly market."

"Blast Dragon for his vagueness." Ranulf's expression tightened with frustration.

"Dragon?" Francis asked.

"My brother. 'Tis the name I always called him. Back at Lyonsbridge he was known as Dragonslayer." His expression softened into a wistful smile. "He was the biggest of us three brothers. He could take on both Thomas and me at once and win the victory two times out of three."

Ranulf straightened up on his stool, realizing with sudden horror that he'd been referring to his brother in the past, as if he was dead. "He could best us both and he will again," he amended. "As soon as I find him."

"I wish I could be of more help." Francis's blue eyes were kind.

"Is there a sheriff in Beauville? Or a magistrate?"

"A sheriff, aye—Charles Guise. He's the sheriff of Beauville, but all know that he's really the chief bully of the liege lord, LeClerc."

"LeClerc?"

"Henri LeClerc, the overlord here. He lives in Darmaux Castle and owns some smaller holdings, as well, including the castle at Mordin."

"And this sheriff—Guise—is his man?"

"Aye. I doubt he'll be able to tell you anything. If a knight such as you describe your brother to be had visited Beauville, we would have heard of it, even here."

"I want to speak with the sheriff, nonetheless, and perhaps I'll try to talk with the baron. And I'll need to buy a new horse and weapons."

"You'd fare more cheaply if you rode as far as Rouen. Beauville has more limited possibilities. But you should be able to find a horse there for the right price."

"I'm not concerned with price. I want to get myself outfitted properly again and get started on my mission. I've delayed long enough. I'll ride to town tomorrow if you'll lend me one of your fine mules."

Francis smiled, but asked, "Are you sure you're well enough?"

"Aye. I've lain abed long enough." Ranulf stood. He *was* anxious to start his inquiries about his brother, but he didn't tell the monk that part of his eagerness was due to a desire to see his beautiful nurse once again.

Francis leaned heavily on a fire iron to boost himself up from the stool. "Very well. I'll meet you at the barn in the morning."

"And you'll give me directions to find Sheriff Guise...and to the home where *she's* staying."

Francis hesitated a long moment, then said, "I

don't go to the town much myself, but, aye, I'll tell you where to find her.''

"Thank you, Brother."

Francis gazed steadily into the younger man's face. "Remember your promise."

"That I won't speak of how she cured me?"

"That you won't speak of her at all once you've left here."

Ranulf frowned. "Though I don't understand the reasoning of it, you have my word."

Francis nodded, but as he turned to bank the fire, his eyes were troubled.

"Well, now, that's an unexpected development," Baron LeClerc said, dismounting from his big destrier. He'd just ridden in from reviewing the Darmaux estates to be greeted by the sheriff and his news. Fortunately for Guise, the ride in the brisk spring air had been good for the baron's temperament.

"I thought it best to come to you for further instructions, your lordship, since you've not wanted us interfering with the abbey in the past."

"No." The baron thought for a moment. "No, I don't want your men going in there." He threw the reins of his horse to a waiting stable lad. "So our informant says that the Englishman is being cared for at the abbey, but he doesn't know why he has come there?''

''He says not. I gather the knight has not been too coherent. He's delirious with fever from the wound.''

The baron gave a sardonic smile. ''So at least your wretched attempt at stopping the man accomplished something, Guise. Is it possible he'll die?''

The sheriff shrugged. ''Our monk didn't know.''

LeClerc drew off his long leather gloves and slapped them across the palm of his hands. ''Keep in touch with the abbey. If the man recovers, I want to know why he's here.''

''Very good, milord. And if he dies?''

''Well, then that'll be the end of it, won't it, you bloody idiot?''

''Aye, milord.'' The sheriff bowed his head, but kept his eyes on LeClerc's back as the baron stalked into Darmaux Castle.

The mule kept a steady but maddeningly slow pace. Once again, Ranulf gave a sigh of regret over his lost stallion. It would be hard to find a horse to match Thunder, especially in this country town. He could see it now in the distance—Beauville, Francis had called it. The monk had explained that the Marchand house was a bit of a distance, up a small road that led north of town.

The ride had given him time to reflect on why he had been so insistent on seeing the girl again. He hadn't thought that anything could deter him from his mission to find Dragon. Perhaps the blow to his head had addled him more than was apparent. That was the only explanation he could think of for this odd obsession.

Then he saw her. She was outside a small cottage, kneeling over a garden whose neat rows had long since been abandoned to run wild. She wore a yellow dress that matched her bright hair, the only splotches of light against the dark, tangled weeds.

His breath caught, and a pulse throbbed in his neck. If the head wound had addled his brain, it had done so in a peculiar way, for he never remembered feeling such an instantaneous response to a woman. Not even at that moment when he had first seen Diana again after he and Dragon returned from the Crusades. Of course, Diana had been running into his brother's arms at the time, oblivious to Ranulf's burning gaze.

His nursing angel was oblivious, too, at the moment, intent on her work. But Ranulf intended to change that. In a moment of painful honesty, he admitted that he had not sought out the maid for the noble purpose of giving her a reward. He'd come because he wanted her for himself.

Chapter Five

Bridget was having difficulty keeping up the resolve and high spirits she'd managed the previous day. Both the Marchands had been up before dawn and had been effusive in their thanks for the hearty morning meal she'd prepared, but after they'd finished eating, the older couple had sat on their little stools by the fire and had promptly nodded off to sleep. Bridget had listened to their gentle snoring with a sigh as she cleaned up the morning dishes. This was not the excitement she'd imagined when she'd thought about life beyond the abbey.

She'd decided to work outdoors, hoping that the sunshine on her face might brighten her humor. She'd already seen that the Marchand garden was in total disarray. Someone had evidently planted earlier in the spring, but since then, the plot had been left to grow into nearly unidentifiable tangles of vegetables and weeds.

She began a ruthless attack on the latter—hacking and pulling, then carefully pouring water from her bucket on the tender shoots she had uncovered. She was so engrossed in the effort that she didn't hear the approach of the mule until it was at the edge of the garden. When she looked up in the middle of watering and saw Ranulf, the pail dropped from her hands, water splashing all around as it hit the ground.

He gave her an engaging grin. "I didn't mean to startle you."

She looked down at the dirt on her skirt, which the soaking had turned to mud. Then she turned back to him with a gasp and blurted, "What are you doing here?"

"I came to talk with you." He swung his leg easily over the swayed back of the mule and jumped to the ground.

Bridget's hands smoothed down her muddy skirt. "You can't have. I mean…you're not supposed to know that I'm here."

He grinned. "Ah, well. I'm a resourceful fellow when it comes to finding runaway angels. It's a specialty of mine."

She could feel the sudden rush of heat draining from her cheeks and struggled to regain control over her voice. "I—I'm not an angel."

"But you *are* a runaway. Why did you run from me at the barn the night before last?"

"Who told you to find me here?" she asked, ignoring his question.

"Brother Francis." At her look of amazement, he continued, "I bullied the information out of him as his penance for lying to me. I'd never known a man of God to tell a falsehood before."

His tone was uncensoring, but Bridget felt the need to defend her beloved guardian. "He did it for my sake."

Ranulf crouched down next to her, his eyes scanning her face. "Why? What is it that makes all of you so afraid that you'll not even tell me your name?"

He was no longer wearing the monk's habit she'd dressed him in that first evening. "You found some clothes," she said, ignoring his question.

He shook his head in resignation at her continued avoidance of his questions, then took a step back and gestured to the rough linen tunic and simple wool hose with a grin. "Francis found them for me. From the odor when I got them, I believe they came from a pig farmer, but I aired them through the night so that you'd not have to hold your nose to talk with me, Angel-of-No-Name."

She laughed in spite of herself. "My name's Bridget," she said.

The words were rewarded with a smile. "Bridget," he repeated, as if the name felt pleasant on his tongue. "Bridget the Angel."

His voice was rich with humor. "Some of the brothers would argue with you. When I was growing up, I'd be more likely called little devil than angel."

"You've been visiting the abbey since childhood, then?"

"Aye, that is—" She paused. For some reason, Francis had revealed her whereabouts to the very stranger who had caused her banishment from the abbey, but he apparently had told Ranulf nothing more about her unusual upbringing. It was a secret she still should keep. "Aye," she ended simply.

He waited for more, but when it became obvious that she was not going to elaborate, he cleared his throat and said, "I came to thank you for my care, and I want to give you a reward for saving my life."

She shook her head. "I need no reward. I'm glad you survived." As she said the words, she realized just how true they were. In spite of her discomfiture, she was fiercely glad that Ranulf was kneeling beside her, nearly healthy and watching her with that roguish smile. She couldn't remember when she'd been so glad about anything.

"Ah, but 'twould be my pleasure to reward you,

Mistress Bridget.'' He cocked his head as an idea seemed to strike him. ''Perhaps you'll accept something from me if I ask you for a further favor.''

She could not break the spell of his gaze. ''What would that favor be?''

He hesitated and glanced toward the door of the cottage. ''Perhaps I should ask permission of your...parents first?''

Bridget felt the heat rising in her cheeks again. ''The Marchands are not my parents. I—I merely live here with them.''

''You are their ward?''

She gave a vague nod, but he did not seem to notice her hesitation.

''I'd like your company for the afternoon,'' he said, standing and reaching for her muddy hands. ''To show me around your Beauville. I need to make some inquiries about buying a horse and other supplies.''

Bridget felt a stirring at the pit of her stomach. What he was asking was impossible. How could she show him around Beauville when she'd never set foot in the place herself? And she knew that the monks had hoped she'd stay hidden away at the Marchands. But the idea of *really* seeing something of the outside world—and in particular seeing it with *him*—had her heart racing with excitement.

''I don't go there...um...often,'' she said.

"You'd do better to find your guide in Beauville itself."

"I can think of no better guide than my very own angel. Please," he coaxed. "You may count it as part of my cure, for in fact I do feel a bit dizzy under this strong sun. I might need some nursing to survive the afternoon."

The entire notion was crazy and dangerous, but completely irresistible. She allowed him to pull her up, muddy hands and all, and said, "I warrant the dizzy one is I, Sir Ranulf, for I believe I shall grant your request. Will you wait here while I change my dress?"

He grinned. "I'll stay planted as firmly as a turnip."

Bridget hesitated a moment more, then, before she could lose her courage, she turned around and raced into the house.

Bridget's first impression was that there was much more color in the town than she had ever seen at the abbey. Though many of the houses were built of the same dull gray fieldstone used at St. Gabriel, surrounding the cottages everything was *colorful.* Laundry lines flapped in the winds with brightly stained fabrics. Children ran back and forth, their towheads reflecting the yellow springtime sun. Along the street were people pushing carts full of vegetables and painted pots and dyed leather shoes and all manner of intriguing wares.

She breathed in a deep gulp of air that smelled of bacon grease and boiling tar and lavender—all at the same time. "Isn't it wonderful?" she said to Ranulf.

He smiled back at her, but looked a little confused at her enthusiasm for what was really just a common scene.

Bridget forced her expression to be more composed, but her eyes still darted avidly here and there, taking in every single sight. This may be her only venture out into the real world, she told herself. She was determined to experience it all.

"According to Brother Francis, the sheriff lives at the other end of town," Ranulf said, looking to her for confirmation.

Bridget nodded vaguely. She had no idea where the sheriff lived, though that would probably seem strange to Ranulf.

They moved down the center of the street and Ranulf took her arm to steer her through the muck left by the busy market traffic. It felt strange to have his strong fingers wrapped around her—strange and comforting.

"No one greets you, Mistress Bridget. Is your town so unfriendly?" Ranulf asked after a few moments.

The couple had caused plenty of stares, but so far no one had said a word to them. Bridget hesitated, then said, "I don't know many people here, Sir Ranulf. I told you that you would find a better guide elsewhere."

"Ah, but not a prettier one. There's not a more lovely face in all the town. I've been checking," he added with a grin.

She didn't know how to respond to either his flattery or his teasing. "I'm sure you would find many pretty girls in Beauville if you looked at the right households."

"Nay, I'm happy with the one I've already found. In fact, I've decided to stop looking." He halted in the middle of the street and cupped his hands alongside his eyes. "See, I've blinders on like a plow horse. Not another pretty face will enter my eyes this day."

She laughed at his silliness. "I can't see that it does any harm to look. Indeed, if you don't, you could venture into one of these muck piles and fall flat on your face." She pulled his hand away from his face with one of hers, and he caught hold of it, refusing to let her go. For a long moment they stood facing each other in the middle of the street, hands clasped.

"We should go. People are staring," Bridget

said. She was surprised to find that her voice came out as a bare whisper.

The smile had dropped off Ranulf's face as he watched her. He looked around as though suddenly remembering where they were. "Aye, I'm sorry." He took the hand he'd been holding and tucked it securely into his arm. This time his voice was serious as he said, "In truth, I need no blinders, angel, for I can see naught but you." Then he turned and led the way down the street.

There was something odd about his lovely nurse, and it was not just the spell she had seemed to cast over him.

For one thing, *no one* spoke to her. How could she have lived in a place her whole life and not be acknowledged by a single person? Beyond that, she appeared to wonder at the most common things. When they had passed the cooper's shop, she'd begged to stop and watch how the man and his young assistant bent the staves around the barrel they were making. It was as if she'd never before seen such a sight. And no one at the cooper's had appeared to know her, either.

By the time they reached the end of the street where they were supposed to find the sheriff's house, Ranulf was thoroughly mystified.

"You do know the sheriff, I suppose?" he asked Bridget.

"Nay."

He turned to face her. "Yet you have lived here your whole life? Have the Marchands kept you hidden away all this time?" he asked in jest, but was surprised to see her face go tense.

"I agreed to come with you today, but I'll have to leave unless you promise not to ask anything more about me," she said stiffly.

"I don't understand—"

"I'm sorry," she interrupted. "Please don't ask any more questions."

The words were determined, but there was fear in her eyes. What had Francis said? Ranulf tried to remember the monk's exact words. Something about Bridget's very life being in danger. He lowered his voice. "Who are you, mistress? What are you afraid of?"

She shook her head. "No questions."

"I only want to help you. You saved my life. I'd like to be able to do something—"

She interrupted him with another firm, "No questions, Sir Ranulf. Or I must leave."

He had no choice other than to comply, but the confrontation had dampened the pleasure he'd been feeling at spending a beautiful morning in the company of a lovely woman. His humor wasn't helped when they discovered that the sheriff had ridden to Darmaux Castle and wasn't expected back until later.

The news was told to them by the sheriff's neighbor, an elderly cobbler who never took his eyes from Bridget's face even while he answered Ranulf's questions.

"I'll have to see the sheriff when he returns," Ranulf told the cobbler. "But in the meantime, I need to purchase a horse. Could you direct us toward the livery?"

"You'd find a better pick of horses in Rouen," the old man said, still staring at Bridget.

"Aye, but I need one to get me that far," Ranulf said patiently. "Surely there must be one for sale here in town."

"Jean the Smithy should have one for you. And weapons, if you're in the market. He fancies himself something of an arms maker."

Bridget's beauty would turn any head, but Ranulf was growing annoyed by the cobbler's rude stare, and he sensed that it was making Bridget uncomfortable. Quickly he obtained directions to the blacksmith's establishment, then put a protective arm around Bridget's back and turned away from the old man with a curt thank-you.

"He looked at me as though my hair had suddenly turned green," Bridget said as they walked away.

Ranulf had had much the same opinion, but he laughed and said, "Perhaps he's not seen such a pretty sight for a long time."

"It made me feel odd."

He gave her arm a squeeze. "Pay no attention. I'm surprised you're not accustomed to men's stares by now."

She shook her head slowly. "Nay, I'm not accustomed to them at all."

Something in the way she said it made Ranulf look down at her sharply. The mystery about Mistress Bridget seemed to deepen the longer he spent with her.

"I wish you'd tell me something more—" he began, but he broke off in mid-sentence to cry "Thunder!"

They were walking up to the big wooden stables that housed the town's prosperous blacksmith. Grazing quietly in a small corral at one side was a cloudy gray stallion. Ranulf dropped his hold on Bridget's arm and took off toward the horse at a run.

The animal gave a whinny at the knight's approach and walked over to meet him at the fence.

Ranulf called back over his shoulder. "It's my horse!"

By the time Bridget reached the fence, Ranulf had boosted himself over it and was standing next to the big animal, rubbing its neck. Thunder tossed his head in acknowledgment.

"Ah, but it's good to see you, boy," Ranulf said. He nodded to Bridget, who was standing a step back, looking hesitant. "He's gentle enough. Here, pat him, if you like."

She put out a tentative hand and touched the big animal's forehead, then smiled. "You're right. The mules would nip at me if I ever tried such a thing."

Ranulf threw an arm over Thunder's neck and dragged himself up on his back. "Not Thunder. I've trained him to be fierce with enemies, but gentle with beautiful women."

"Only with the beautiful ones?"

"Aye." Ranulf grinned. "The ugly ones he bites."

Bridget shook her head, laughing, then asked, "But how did he come to be here? Is this the animal that the robbers took from you?"

Ranulf's grin faded. "Aye." He gave Thunder a final pat, then slid down from his back. "I should check him over to see that he's none the worse for our encounter, then I intend to have a discussion with the smithy about where he came from."

"The smithy might well make the same inquiry

of you," boomed a voice from the entrance to the barn.

Bridget and Ranulf turned around to see a giant man nearly filling the oversize wooden door. He wore a leather apron over his hose and nothing more, leaving his shoulders and arms bare. They bulged with muscle. His head was bald and glistened in the sunlight.

"Would you be Jean the Smithy?" Ranulf asked without alarm.

"Aye." The big man moved forward and it seemed as if the ground shook with each step. "Who the devil are you and why are you making yourself free with my horse?"

Ranulf smiled and offered a hand. "It was a reunion of sorts. *Your* horse and I are old acquaintances."

After a moment's hesitation, the blacksmith reached out and shook the offered hand. Though Ranulf's hand was big, the smith's engulfed it.

"Well, the horse is mine now," the smith said.

"Would you mind if I inquired as to how you came by the animal?" Ranulf asked.

Bridget watched the exchange with interest. In his own way, the big, earthy blacksmith was as fascinating as Ranulf to someone who had seen nothing but monks all her life.

"Aye, I'd mind," he answered gruffly. "Folks

around here don't much like strangers who come around asking questions.''

Bridget thought she could notice a tightening of Ranulf's jaw, but his voice was still pleasant as he said, "If you came by him honestly, I've no quarrel with you. But I'd like to buy him.''

"The horse is not for sale.''

Neither man blinked as they sized each other up for a long moment. Bridget cleared her throat and addressed the big man. "This horse was taken from Sir Ranulf by outlaws. You should be grateful that he's offering to buy it back rather than demand it as his due.''

Ranulf shot her a surprised glance, and the blacksmith turned his gaze on her for the first time. "Who are you?'' he barked.

Bridget swallowed. "I—who I am is not important. The issue is the horse, which should be returned to its rightful owner.''

The smithy stood eyeing them both. "Sir Ranulf?'' he asked. "Are you truly a knight?''

"Aye,'' Ranulf answered. "And that truly is my horse.''

"You don't much look the gentlemen in those clothes, but if the horse is yours, I'd wager you're not a peasant. He's the finest piece of horseflesh I've seen in these parts.''

"Thank you. He's served me well.''

"But he's mine now. I bought him fair and square."

· She could see the carefully banked excitement in Ranulf's eyes as he said, "I'll pay you a fair price for my horse, and I'll double it if you can lead me to the man who sold it to you."

The smithy's eyes grew wide. All hostility had disappeared from his tone as he said, "I can tell you who brought in the animal, but he was no bandit. It was one of the baron's men."

"And which baron would that be?" Ranulf asked.

"Henri LeClerc, Baron of Darmaux. And lest you think the baron's an outlaw, I'll tell you that his liege lord is the Duke of Austria."

"Who's the Duke of Austria?" Bridget asked.

Both men looked a little surprised at her question, but Ranulf answered, "He's one of the most powerful men on the continent. He's the one who seized King Richard the Lionhearted as he returned from Crusade and held him prisoner. My brother Thomas and I were among those who collected the ransom to free him."

"So 'tis not likely that this baron or his duke would have wanted to rob you?" she asked.

Ranulf shook his head slowly. "The duke has more arms than any noble in Europe. I can't imagine what interest he would have in a poor English knight.''

''I told you the information would be of little use,'' Jean said with a shrug. ''But I'll take that fair price you're offering me on the horse and an extra gold piece bonus for my trouble, as well.''

''Agreed,'' Ranulf said, extending his hand once again. The blacksmith invited them into his shed, where soon he and Ranulf were engrossed in the smithy's collection of armaments. It reminded Bridget of the monks discussing their labors in the work shed and she stood by silently while Ranulf agreed to the purchase of a sword, a small buckler and a leather helmet.

Once the blacksmith had seen Ranulf's gold, he had become completely agreeable. As they settled the terms, Ranulf spotted an unusual black helmet sitting on a shelf. ''What's that one?'' he asked.

The blacksmith smiled broadly. '''Tis a wondrous thing, made of a metal like none you've ever seen, I vow.'' He lifted the helmet from its place, then smashed it against a nearby anvil. It rang like a church bell.

''You've ruined it,'' Ranulf exclaimed.

''Nay.'' Jean's big mouth spread in a grin. ''See for yourself.''

He held the helmet toward Ranulf, who took it and turned it around in his hands with a low whistle. "Not even a dent," he said. The black metal triggered a vague memory. "What's it made of?"

Jean shrugged. "'Tis something new."

Ranulf turned the helmet over, studying it. "Perhaps I should have this one, then, instead of the leather."

"I can't sell you that one."

"Why not?"

"'Tis promised to another customer."

"I'll pay you a higher price."

The smithy looked uneasy. "I beg pardon, sir, but I simply cannot sell it to you."

Ranulf studied it a minute more, then reached to put it back on the shelf. "No matter, then. I'll take the leather."

"Very good," the smithy said, relieved. "I'll get everything cleaned up and polished for you."

Bridget had been left standing for some time. "Good," Ranulf said briskly. "I'll take the horse and saddle now, and be back for the weapons later."

"Aye, I'll have them for you on the morrow, milord." His eyes slid to Bridget. "Be this your lady?"

Bridget flushed. "Nay," she said before Ranulf could answer.

Ranulf looked from Bridget to Jean with some puzzlement. "Mistress Bridget lives here in Beauville," he said. "I'm surprised you don't know each other."

One of Jean's bushy brown eyebrows shot up, pushing the skin of his forehead up toward his bald head. "I thought I knew everyone in Beauville."

Bridget's chin went up. "I—I've only just arrived," she said. "I've come to live with my aunt and uncle, the Marchands."

The answer seemed to satisfy the blacksmith, but Ranulf shot her a questioning look. It took several more minutes for the transaction to be completed, but finally the deal was struck, Thunder was saddled and they took their leave of the smithy.

Ranulf, leading Thunder behind him, lapsed into silence as they walked down the road. Bridget sensed that his earlier lighthearted mood had changed, and she had a feeling that it had something to do with their final exchange with the blacksmith.

Finally she said, "What a lucky thing that you got your horse back."

"Aye," he said.

She waited a minute or two, then tried again. "I suspect you're eager to ride him again."

"Nay, the walk is good on such a fine day."

Bridget frowned. The exuberance of the fine day was fading for her, and she realized that her spirits had more to do with Ranulf's company than with the bright weather. Now that he suddenly seemed withdrawn, it was as if clouds had covered the sun.

Chapter Six

She was still lying, Ranulf thought with a twinge of sadness. He'd hoped that she had begun to trust him, that whatever secrets she was trying to hide would not interfere with their developing attraction for each other, which she surely must be feeling as strongly as he was. But she'd told him that the Marchands were no relation to her, and she'd just told the blacksmith that they were her aunt and uncle. What possible reason would she have to lie about something so simple? *No questions,* she had said.

He gave a distracted answer to another of her questions about Thunder, then looked at her in surprise as she stopped, pulled on his arm and asked in a loud voice, "Are you angry with me?"

Her irritation heightened the natural color of her cheeks. "Nay," he said with a sigh.

"I suspect it wasn't pleasant to pay good money for a horse that was already rightly yours."

"I don't care about the money."

Her eyes were concerned. "What, then? You looked distressed just now."

If he told her that his concern was for her, he was afraid their day together would be over. Mustering a smile, he said, "I'm frustrated that I have to wait to speak with the sheriff. I've come to Normandy looking for my brother, a quest that has already been delayed by circumstances beyond my control. Now it appears that the search will have to wait even longer."

As they continued walking down a shady side street in the general direction of the Marchand cottage, he told her briefly about Dragon's disappearance and the letter that brought him to St. Gabriel.

Comprehension dawned in her eyes. "So it *was* a dragon you were calling for when you were in the delirium."

"I wouldn't be surprised," he answered. "Edmund is on my mind most of the time."

"And the lady—this Diana? You called for her, too."

Ranulf blinked and had a sudden, hazy memory of calling out to Diana, then *kissing her.* But it hadn't been Diana he had kissed. "Aye, she is Edmund's promised bride."

In what he was sure was an unconscious gesture, Bridget lifted her hand briefly to her lips. "Is she a fine lady?" she asked. "Like Guinevere?"

Ranulf laughed. "So you know of Guinevere, eh? The beautiful downfall of brave King Arthur. I *hope* Diana's not such a one as she. I'd not see my brother matched to such a weak spirit."

"Nay, Guinevere was not weak. She was a woman who had been given one lot in life and found the courage to seek a greater happiness."

"She betrayed Arthur."

"But by staying with Arthur, she was betraying her own true spirit. Her dilemma came because she wanted to find her own path without hurting anyone else, and that's not always possible."

Ranulf stopped walking and looked at his companion in wonder. How did a young woman who had been raised in a simple farm village become educated enough to discuss literature and philosophy? "Do you read, mistress?" he asked her.

"Aye." At his puzzled look, she continued, "The monks taught me. I spend a great deal of time in the library at St. Gabriel."

Ranulf shook his head. "I've only known a few women in my life who read."

"Is your grandmother Ellen one of them?"

The name made him smile. "Aye, and she would no doubt agree with you about Guinevere, for she's

ever been one to say that a woman should have as
much right as a man to determine her destiny.''

''I would like your grandmother.''

''Aye. She would like you as well.''

They lapsed into silence for a moment as each
realized the improbability of simple Bridget of
Beauville ever meeting the grand Lady of Lyonsbridge. But the discussion had restored Ranulf's
good humor. ''Do you have to go back home right
away?'' he asked. ''Will your *aunt and uncle* be
looking for you?''

She didn't seem to notice his sarcastic tone.
''Nay. I told them I'd be back before dusk.''

They'd reached the far end of town where the
small weekly market was set up behind the church.
''Good. Shall we see what delicacies the good merchants of Beauville have to offer? You must be
hungry by now.'' He gestured toward the ramshackle row of market stands.

Bridget hesitated only a moment, then said, with
a little grin, ''The truth is, I'm famished.''

Ranulf grinned back at her. ''We'll find something for you, too, Thunder,'' he told his horse,
tying him to the church hitching post. Then he
seized her hand and they headed off in the direction
of the market.

Bridget knew she shouldn't risk a trip through
the busy marketplace. It was bad enough that she'd

had people in the town staring as they walked through, the sheriff's neighbor looking at her as if she were a ghost and the blacksmith questioning where she'd come from. Now she was faced with more close encounters with Beauville merchants as Ranulf led her along the row of stands.

He was the one who caught their eye first, especially in the case of the women. Tall and handsome, even in the pig farmer's clothes he carried himself with the bearing of a warrior. But eventually the merchants would turn to look at her, and at each stop they were met with puzzled looks.

They skipped over the butcher's table with its string of hares dressed and dancing in the breeze and went directly to a row of hot treats where Ranulf pulled out some copper coins to purchase a fruit-filled pastry for each of them. Ignoring the stares of the baker, Bridget bit into the sugary treat with relish.

Ranulf chuckled at her enthusiasm. "You should have told me you were starving, mistress. I'd not thought about feeding you because I figured that angels didn't require earthly food."

"This angel does," Bridget said, sucking air into her mouth to keep from burning herself on the hot filling.

Ranulf made short work of his pastry, finishing

it in two giant bites. "That will do for a start," he said, and reached for Bridget's hand to pull her farther along the aisle.

Soon Ranulf spotted a leather stand. He walked over to it and picked up a small pouch. "You wear no purse, Mistress Bridget," he said. "Where do you keep your coin?"

Bridget hesitated. She didn't keep her coins anywhere for the simple reason that she'd never in her life possessed one. "I wasn't expecting to need any today," she said.

"Nor do you," he assured her. "But ladies like to pick out new things. Let me buy you a purse."

She shook her head. "There's no need," she told him.

He put down the first one he'd selected and reached for another at the back of the table. It was dyed red and had the picture of a rose etched on the front. "This one, I think," he said, studying it carefully.

Bridget went to stand beside him and looked down at the tiny bag. She'd never in her life owned anything like it, but she shook her head once more. "Really, I don't need it."

The young boy who was minding the booth stood at eager attention, conscious that he was about to make a sale. "It be the prettiest of the lot. And the dearest," he added slyly.

Ranulf handed the boy a coin, then turned to Bridget. "It loops around like this, see?" He reached down to her waist to tuck the flap of the purse around her belt. She had to force herself not to jump at the unaccustomed feeling of a man's fingers sliding against her stomach.

When the purse was fastened to his satisfaction, Ranulf pulled back to survey his handiwork. "There," he said. "Do you like it?"

She looked down at the little pouch. "Aye," she said in a small voice.

He nodded, then seized her hand to continue down the row of stalls. They stopped for a meat pie, then a glass of mulled wine. Finally, at the end of the row, Ranulf stopped in front of an old woman who sat behind a huge wheel of cheese. "Good afternoon, mistress," he said to her. "Do you think you could cut off a hunk of your fine-looking cheese for this pretty lady and myself?"

Unlike the sellers in the other stalls, the woman had glanced only briefly at Ranulf, then turned her gaze on Bridget. "By the blessed Virgin!" she said, crossing herself.

Ranulf looked down at Bridget, who seemed to be mystified by the woman's reaction. For a moment no one spoke while the woman continued to stare as though she were, in fact, seeing a vision of the Virgin herself. Bridget shifted uncomfortably under the scrutiny.

After a moment, Ranulf asked, "Is the cheese not for sale?"

The woman turned back to look at him. "Be ye one of them?" she asked, her jaw trembling with the weakness of age.

Ranulf and Bridget exchanged a glance. Perhaps the woman was not of sound mind. "One of whom, good mother?" Ranulf asked gently.

"The evil ones," she croaked. "The baron's men."

Bridget moved around the edge of the stall and went on her knees beside the old woman, who was growing agitated. She took one of her blue-veined hands and stroked it. "No one is evil here. Sir Ranulf is a good knight who has been on holy Crusade. He's here searching for his brother."

A small stream of spittle started from the corner of the woman's mouth as she lifted her hand free and touched Bridget's cheek. "You must find a place to hide, child, for your sake and the babe's, as well. They'll kill you both."

Bridget looked up at Ranulf, who shook his head helplessly. "Perhaps we'd best move on," he said.

But Bridget stayed where she was. There seemed to be a genuine gleam of recognition in the woman's faded blue eyes. "Do you think you know me?" she asked.

The old lady nodded and said again, "You must hide from them, Charlotte, and protect the baby at all costs."

Obviously the woman was confusing her with someone else, but with sudden excitement, Bridget realized that the confusion might have something to do with her past. "Who is Charlotte, mother?" she asked.

But the older woman had become too agitated to make sense.

"Pay her no mind," said a pleasant voice from behind her. A man was walking up to the stall, a crate full of eggs in his arms. "I'm sorry, I had to step away for a moment," he said, giving a small bow of his head to first Bridget, then Ranulf. "Just let me put this down and I'll be happy to serve you."

Bridget gave the woman's hand a final pat, then stood and stepped back from the stall. The old cheese seller's eyes had closed and she was rocking back and forth, crooning tunelessly. "I'm Pierre Courmier," the newcomer introduced himself. "This is Camille, my grandmother," he explained. "She doesn't make much sense anymore, but she likes to come out on market day and see the townsfolk. Even with her memory gone, she can still greet everyone in Beauville by their name.''

"She called me Charlotte,'' Bridget said.

Pierre frowned. ''That's odd.'' He squinted to see her face. ''But you're not from here.''

Bridget looked at Ranulf, then said, ''No.''

Pierre was shaking his head. ''I don't remember anyone in Beauville with the name of Charlotte. Probably someone she knew in the past.'' The matter seemed unimportant to him. ''Would you like to sample some cheese?''

Ranulf took out his coins and purchased a slice for each of them.

"Where are you folks from?'' the dairyman asked with a friendly smile.

Ranulf looked from the old lady to her grandson and finally to Bridget. ''That's exactly what I'm beginning to wonder,'' he said.

Pierre looked confused.

"Sir Ranulf is a knight, back from the Crusades,'' Bridget answered quickly.

Pierre gave a skeptical glance at Ranulf's clothes, then shrugged. ''Ah. Well, remember if you need any dairy products, come to the Courmier family. Our farm is just out of town, beyond the Marchand place. Do you know them?''

Bridget gave a nervous nod, popped the last bite

of her cheese slice into her mouth and said to Ranulf, "I should be getting back."

Ranulf thanked the dairyman, then followed Bridget without a word down the aisle of stalls and back to the church where they had left Thunder.

By the time they reached the horse, the silence between them had once again become awkward. She barely knew the English knight, Bridget thought. She owed him no explanation, and there was no reason for her to place the abbey at risk by telling her secrets. But she could tell that he was hurt and perhaps angry at her deceptions, and she found herself wanting to put things right between them.

He didn't look at her as he untied Thunder. "Would you like to ride back to your—to the Marchand house?" he asked stiffly.

"I suppose you wonder why you've heard different versions of my story today."

He threw the reins over Thunder's neck. "If you've no desire to tell me, there's nothing I can do about it. 'No questions,' you said."

"Aye."

"So would you like to ride?"

She eyed the big horse doubtfully, then said with an attempt at a smile, "I suppose 'tis just like being up on Snail, only higher."

Making no response to her attempt at lightheart-edness, he swung himself up on the horse and reached an arm down to her. "Put your foot on top of mine and let me pull you up," he directed.

He lifted her easily into the saddle in front of him and settled her in his arms. The sensation was warm and pleasant, but as they rode out of town toward the Marchand cottage, once again she felt the weight of his silence.

"Are you angry, Ranulf?" she asked.

He made no reply.

"You *are* angry."

His arms tensed, then he turned her around to face him, and said, "Should I be angry? You told me that the Marchands were no relation. Then you told the blacksmith that you are their niece. You claimed to be from Beauville, then told the dairy-man that you are not. Have I yet today heard you utter a single true thing?"

His face looked angry, but in his eyes she could read hurt, and it was the hurt that was her undoing. She took in a deep, shaky breath and said, "I'm sorry."

"You admit you've lied?"

She nodded.

"Why? Surely you can't think I would do any-thing to hurt you. You saved my life."

"I'm not worried about myself. My concern is for...others who might be hurt because of me."

Slowly comprehension dawned in his eyes. "It's the abbey, isn't it? You're protecting the monks."

Now it was Bridget's turn to look scared. "St. Gabriel could be disbanded if anyone found out."

"That you live there?" Ranulf confirmed.

"Aye. St. Gabriel is my home."

"How long have you been there?"

She met his direct gaze. "As long as I can remember."

"Years?" he asked in amazement.

She twisted around to face the road ahead, then responded, "My whole life."

Ranulf was silent a long moment. "But surely you've traveled about, visited the town..." His voice trailed off as she started shaking her head.

They'd almost reached the place where a smaller road branched off the main. Opposite the fork was a stand of trees ending at a gently sloping bank that led to a small stream. Ranulf steered Thunder off the road toward the water.

"Where are we going?" Bridget asked.

He didn't answer, but let Thunder take a few more steps until they reached the edge of the trees. Then he lifted her up and reached over the horse to deposit her on the grass, before jumping to the ground himself.

"We'll let Thunder drink some water," he said, leading the horse down the bank. All traces of anger were gone from his tone and, when he turned back to her, his expression was unreadable.

He motioned to a level place at the top of the bank and, when she sat down, dropped beside her. Finally he turned and took both her hands in his. "Let's start from the beginning. If you live at the abbey, why did I find you at the Marchand cottage?"

Now that he knew as much as he did, Bridget could see no further reason for deception. "The monks sent me there the morning after we spoke in the barn. They were afraid of what would happen if you discovered me."

"But how did you come to live at the abbey in the first place? Didn't you have parents? Family?"

"Just the monks."

"What a strange life for a young girl."

"Aye, but I've never been unhappy."

Ranulf sat for a moment, digesting the revelation, then asked, "And you've never been in Beauville before today?"

"Never. Nor anywhere else but St. Gabriel."

"But the old woman looked as though she recognized you."

"She couldn't have. I've never seen her before, and, remember, she called me by another name."

"Charlotte, was it not? Do you know any such person?"

She shook her head. "I don't know anyone except the monks."

Ranulf smiled. "You know me now."

"Aye, I know you."

"No wonder we got nothing but stares. I wager 'tis not every day the good people of Beauville see a strange English knight dressed as a pig farmer and a beautiful unknown angel come strolling through their town."

Bridget returned his smile, then looked away at the rushing stream below them. "You must stop calling me an angel," she said. "You're not delirious anymore."

"Nay, but your beauty is no less heavenly than it appeared in the midst of my fever."

There was a husky tone to his voice that set a hum stirring in Bridget's midsection. With a sudden burst of daring, she said, "'Twas the fever made you kiss me, though."

"Mayhap. I would not otherwise be so ungrateful as to take liberties with a woman who was saving my life. I apologize for having done so.''

He had dropped his hold on her hands, which had grown cold without the warmth of his touch. She rubbed them together. '''Twas no great harm,'' she said.

He bent his head to try to see into her averted eyes. ''But if you've lived at the abbey your entire life, then that was your first kiss?''

''Aye, and my last, I expect. Once I go back to St. Gabriel, the monks will be careful to keep me away from future visitors.''

''Go back!'' Ranulf's exclamation was loud enough to make Thunder toss his head and turn to look at his master to see what was amiss. The knight continued in a lower tone. ''You would go back there to live isolated in such a way?''

''It's my home,'' Bridget said. ''It's all I've ever known, and, as I said, the monks are my family.''

''But you are a lovely young woman. You should be meeting people—young men who will court you and offer you a life and a family of your own. You should be having that *real* first kiss and many more to follow it.''

Bridget smiled. ''It was real enough.''

He seized her shoulders and turned her to face him. ''Nay, it was not,'' he said firmly. ''A real kiss is not a fumbled gesture in the dark between strangers. It's—'' he searched for the words ''—it's an expression two people use when their hearts are too full to put it any other way.''

Her eyes misted. Down the bank, Thunder shifted his feet and gave a whinny of impatience, but it seemed as if the sound came from a great distance. ''Tis something I'll never have then.''

He raised a callused finger and wiped a tear that had started down her cheek. ''Aye, you will, angel,'' he said. Then he lowered his lips to hers.

Chapter Seven

It was the last thing Ranulf had intended. He'd wanted to reward his lifesaving healer, not take advantage of her innocence for his own pleasure. But there had been a slight trembling to her lips when she'd said she would never truly have her first kiss, and he'd known instantly that he had to be the one to give it to her.

She'd had as strange a life as he could imagine and had told him that she was soon to return to it, but first he could show her the magic that was possible between a man and a maid. He'd do it for her sake—and because he could no more stop himself than he could stop the stream at their feet from flowing.

She turned readily into his kiss with a sweet sigh of acceptance. Her lips were moist and lush and his body responded with instantaneous arousal, but he

willed himself to restraint. For several long moments, he didn't even touch her except with his
mouth. He made his kisses gentle and slow, with
only a tantalizing, occasional stroke of his tongue.
Then she made a kind of whimper in the back of
her throat, and he reached to pull her onto his lap,
at the same time deepening the onslaught of his
mouth over hers.

She responded by wrapping her arms around his
neck and pressing him close, bringing the hardened
tips of her breasts against the soft jersey of the pig
farmer's tunic.

She moved with the rhythm of their kisses, wrig-
gling her bottom against his wool hose. Ranulf felt
sudden lust pounding through his center, and he
pulled back.

She lay in his arms, cheeks flushed, lips swollen,
and gave him a sleepy, contented smile. "Thank
you," she whispered.

Ranulf laughed. "'Tis the gentleman who does
the thanking, angel."

"Why, if 'tis of equal pleasure to the lady?"

Ranulf considered for a moment. "I'm not sure.
I believe it's assumed that in lovemaking the gentleman reaps the greater reward."

She pulled herself up and slipped off his lap to
the grass. "Did you like it, too, then?"

Ranulf rolled his eyes. "Aye."

"I'm glad. But I still think it was very kind of you."

"*Kind* of me," Ranulf repeated dryly.

"To take pity on me and assure that I would not live out my years without knowing what it was like."

"It had nothing to do with pity."

"But you wanted me to have a real kiss, right? That's why you did it?"

Ranulf made a sound of exasperation. "Aye, I wanted you to have a real kiss, but I also *wanted to kiss you.*"

She didn't look entirely convinced, but she leaned back on her hands and closed her eyes with a happy smile, as though still savoring the experience. "I'm glad you wanted to. And I'm glad it was you. And it *was* lovely."

Ranulf shook his head in bewilderment. Though he was not the ladies' man his brother Thomas had been before he'd met his Alyce Rose, Ranulf had kissed a number of women in his twenty-six years. But he'd never before known a woman to react quite like Bridget. She was the one experiencing something new, yet she seemed in utter control of the situation, while he sat there with his insides shaking with unsatisfied desire and his mind a-jumble.

"Aye, it was good," he agreed after a moment.

''Yet you would give up all that for a world behind the walls of St. Gabriel?''

She opened her eyes and her smile faded. ''I have no other home.''

He frowned. ''Haven't you ever tried to find out about your real family?''

''I used to ask as a child, but I haven't for years. I only remember that my inquiries always led to worried looks and hushed conferences among the monks, so I stopped making them. They've been good to me, and I'd not hurt them for the world.''

Ranulf felt a stab of frustration at the good brothers of St. Gabriel. They seemed to be well-intentioned, but they didn't have the right to deprive a young woman of all the world had to offer.

''You could ask more questions about the old woman who thought she recognized you. The sheriff's neighbor, as well. I'd thought his stares were due to your beauty, but perhaps he thought he'd recognized you, too.''

Bridget shook her .head vigorously. ''Nay, I should not have ventured into town at all. I believe the monks thought that I would stay safely tucked away at the Marchands' until it was safe for me to return.''

''After I left.''

''Aye. And now that Brother Francis has told you about me, I suspect I could go back to the abbey with you this afternoon." She gave a little frown. "Are you going back?"

"Aye, they've agreed to let me finish my recuperation there." He lifted a hand to his bandage.

"Oh!" she exclaimed. "I'd almost forgotten about your head. It's not hurting? We didn't injure it more a few minutes ago when we, ah…when we were…"

"Locked in each other's arms?" he finished with a smile. "No, 'tis not my head, precisely, that's hurting after our encounter."

She didn't seem to understand his reference and Ranulf gave his head a little shake. He'd not been with a woman in months, and now that he found one to whom he was instantly attracted, she turned out to be not only innocent, but most likely totally unaware of what went on between a man and a maid. His code of honor would tell him to get up on Thunder and ride away from St. Gabriel as fast as the swift horse could take him.

Instead, he said, "I'll gladly take you back, but I'm not sure what will happen if we ride there together. Francis specifically had me promise that I wouldn't tell the others that I had seen you."

Bridget pursed her lips. "Aye, 'twould cause a scandal no doubt. I'm not supposed to see you, either. Brother Alois, our abbot, would have me on

my knees saying penance for the next week if he
knew we'd spent an entire afternoon together.''

''If you stay at the Marchands', I could come to
see you again tomorrow when I seek out the sheriff.''

Her breasts seemed to rise and fall more quickly,
while his own breathing stopped entirely while he
waited for her answer. Finally she said, ''I'd like
that.''

''The Marchands will not object?'' he asked.

She shook her head. ''They're lost in their own
small world. They barely seem to notice that I've
arrived.''

Across the stream, the sun was low in the sky.
Ranulf jumped up and extended his hand to help
her up. ''Then I'll take you back now, and see you
in the morning. If the sheriff still hasn't returned,
you can help me pass the day on a pleasant ride
through this Norman countryside of yours.''

Bridget looked around at the peaceful scene.
''My countryside has never been anything but the
land directly surrounding the abbey,'' she said, letting him pull her up. ''We'll see this for the first
time together.''

The old shoemaker pulled on his cap and scraped
his feet nervously in the dust as the man who had
ridden in beside the sheriff of Beauville asked him

for the third time, "Did this stranger tell you why he was searching out the sheriff?"

The cobbler shook his head without looking up into the big man's odd violet eyes.

"His head was bandaged, you say? But he appeared to be in good health?"

The old man nodded. "He walked right enough, milord. His boots were of poor quality." The man gave a little tisk. "Shoddy workmanship."

"I don't care about the man's boots, you fool," the nobleman barked. "Tell me about the girl."

"The spitting image, she was, your lordship. The spitting image of the lady Charlotte."

The nobleman turned to the sheriff. "Can we believe what this dunderhead is telling us, Guise? Was this truly Charlotte's brat wandering around the town?"

Before the sheriff could reply, the old cobbler himself answered, "I used to fit her shoes, milord, the lady Charlotte's. She came right here to my shop, and I never saw the likes for beauty. A right angel, she was, her ladyship." He lifted his head while he made a hasty sign of the cross, then turned his gaze back down to the ground.

"He speaks the truth, milord," the sheriff confirmed. "I was just a lad, but I still remember the lady Charlotte's visits to town. She always had a kind word and a smile for the humblest among us.

I reckon there are a number of the older folks who remember her.''

"Aye, but this was not the lady Charlotte who's been dead these many years,'' the cobbler said. "The girl I saw was no ghost. She was as near to me as your lordship and I looked right into her eyes—spun gold, they were, just like the lady Charlotte's.''

LeClerc glared at the bowed head of the cobbler. "Did you speak to her of the resemblance?''

"No, your lordship.''

His companion scowled. "I knew this would come back to haunt me some day. I should have never agreed to let the child live.''

"Do you suppose this means that our monk has broken his agreement—'' the sheriff began.

"I don't like to *suppose,* Guise. I depend on those who expect my favor to provide me with the facts.''

"Aye, milord.''

LeClerc looked at the cobbler. "Have you spoken of this to anyone?''

The shoemaker's gaze was fearful as he looked up at the baron, then over at the sheriff, whose hand was on the heavy knife in his belt. "Nay, nor will I ever, I swear, your lordship.''

LeClerc hesitated, but finally said to the sheriff,

"Let him go for now. If you hear that his tongue has been wagging, cut it out."

The cobbler gave one more scraping bow, then scurried away.

Guise shifted uncomfortably. "I'd have sworn by the devil's eyeballs that I killed the knave."

"Could it be another?" the baron asked.

"With a bandaged head? Nay, it must be he."

The baron slapped a riding whip onto his own thigh. "I want to know where he is and why he was riding to St. Gabriel in the first place."

"I'll do my best, milord. What about the girl?"

LeClerc's eyes narrowed to purple slits. "It may be time to rid ourselves of that particular problem."

"He's a handsome one, that lad of yours," old Mistress Marchand said with a little sigh, leaning back on her stool to rest against the cold stone wall of the cottage.

Bridget finished shelling the last of the peas she'd salvaged from the Marchand garden. She would put them on to soak before she left this morning with Ranulf and they'd be ready to cook on her return. "Oh, Sir Ranulf is not my lad, Claudine. He's a stranger I helped nurse at the abbey."

"At the abbey. Brother Ebert wouldn't say much when he came to ask if you could stay here, but

I've wanted to ask you, child. Whatever was a young lass like yourself doing at St. Gabriel?''

Bridget had already discovered that the Marchands had been told little of her story, and, if she intended to go back to live at the abbey, she suspected that it was best to leave things that way. "I'd lost my family," she replied vaguely. That much was true enough.

Claudine's faded eyes grew moist. "Ah, you poor mite. Well, 'tis as I told Brother Ebert, you're welcome to stay here as long as you like. And you can bring your young man around."

"He's not my young man," Bridget repeated patiently.

But Mistress Marchand did not appear to absorb the words. Her eyes closed and she said dreamily, "I remember the days when Philip used to come courting. All those years ago…yet it could have been only yesterday." She opened her eyes and looked at Bridget. "He was tall and handsome in those days. Full of pretty speeches and fancy ways. Ah, you should've seen my Philip back then, Bridget."

Bridget smiled. "And you're still in love after all these years."

"Aye. Once a heart is set to the perfect tune, it's like the nightingale—it'll sing nothing but that one song its whole life."

Now Bridget's eyes misted. "You're lucky."

"Aye, that we are—Philip and I. Though it seems harder these days." She looked around the little cottage, which had been greatly improved by Bridget's labors. "The truth is, we've lived our three score years and more. Philip is tired." She gazed toward the bed in the far corner of the room where her husband was still sleeping. Her eyes brimmed with love tinged with sadness.

"You take good care of him," Bridget said gently.

The old woman simply shook her head.

"It was kind of you to agree to have me, adding to your troubles," Bridget added.

"Lord, child, you've been nothing but a help. You've cleaned my house, weeded the garden, cooked that delicious stew yesterday. We haven't been this well tended since my daughter married and left for Rouen. Still—" her gaze made a slow tour of the cozy room "—it makes a body feel kind of useless not to be able to keep things up anymore."

Bridget was unsure how to respond. "I'm glad I could help," she said finally.

Claudine sat up straighter and forced a smile. "Ah, child, you don't need to be sitting here listening to a whining old woman. Go pretty yourself up for that young man of yours."

"He's, ah, he's not my young—"

Claudine no longer seemed to be listening. She leaned back against the wall again and closed her eyes. "Young love is a wonderful thing. Aye, Philip and I had that once. There was not a lad in the village could hold a candle to Philip Marchand when it came to pretty speeches...."

Her head drooped a little, and it appeared that the old woman had fallen asleep. Bridget considered briefly whether she should try to move her from the stool so that she wouldn't topple over, but she decided to leave her alone. The morning nap had evidently become a ritual for the older couple, as had most of their daily routine.

Bridget sat watching them both for a long moment, wondering what it would be like to have a partner to share all the everyday moments of life as the months and seasons and years marched by. She would have the monks, she supposed, though it wasn't quite the same.

She stood quietly and went out of the cottage, leaving the two asleep. It was another beautiful spring day. She looked down the path to the road from where he'd be coming. A now familiar hum of excitement tingled in her midsection. She walked to the little well behind the house and drew herself some water to freshen up with. Ranulf may not be her "young man," as she had tried to make clear to Claudine Marchand, but he *was* every bit as handsome as the old lady had said. And he *was* coming to spend the day with her.

Soon he would be riding out of her life, but for today, if she pleased, she could pretend that he was a young man come courting, just as Philip Marchand had courted his Claudine all those years ago. She wagered that Ranulf Brand could muster some pretty speeches, too, when he was of a mind.

Smiling at her own fantasy, she cupped her hands into the bucket of water and gave herself a cold splash in the face.

"The sheriff was away again," Ranulf explained as he dismounted from Thunder in front of the cottage. "And the cobbler's shop was barred, so I'm afraid my questions will have to wait one more day."

Bridget found it difficult to restrain the smile that met his words. "I'm glad we shall have our ride," she said.

"Aye." Ranulf's smile was equally broad. "Though I'm feeling guilty that I've wasted so much time inquiring about Dragon. If the sheriff hasn't returned by tomorrow, I may have to ride to Rouen."

"You weren't wasting time—you were recovering. In fact, I doubt you should be contemplating

such a trip even now. You must let me see how
your wound is faring.''

Ranulf seized the hand she was lifting to his
head. ''My wound is fine, thanks to a brilliant nurse
who used to creep in to tend me in the middle of
the night.'' He kissed the tips of her fingers.
''Which reminds me that I've yet to give her a
reward.''

''She needs none, but she would like to be sure
that her medicines have completed their task.''

Ranulf shook his head. ''It's fine—nearly healed.
I keep the bandage only to avoid scaring little children along the road. I'm afraid the incident has left
my skull a bit altered.''

''It will all return to rights eventually.''

Ranulf grinned. ''I'm glad to hear it, but I don't
mind the scar. When I find Dragon, I'll use it to
taunt him over what I've suffered for his negligence
in staying away so long.''

Bridget had heard enough about the holy Crusades to know that many hundreds of soldiers had
never returned. If Ranulf's brother had been missing for three years, it was not too likely that he
would ever be found, but she was not about to argue with his unshakable belief that he would find
his brother alive.

''I daresay, he may have a few scars of his own
to share,'' she said simply.

"He'd better have scars or some other damn good excuse for putting us all through such worry." Ranulf glanced at the door to the cottage. "Do you have to tell the Marchands that you are leaving?"

Bridget shook her head. "They're both asleep. But Mistress Marchand knows that I was to go with you this morning. She called you my 'young man.'"

Ranulf grinned. "Why, she's right. At least, I'm a young man…and I'm all yours for today, fair lady."

"For today," Bridget repeated.

"Aye," he said, and his grin died.

In all of her reading from the special closet at the library, Bridget had never quite imagined *this*. She hadn't realized what it would feel like to ride on the back of a horse with her arms clasped around a man's strong chest, to laugh with him as they crossed meadows smelling of springtime and splashed through shallow streams.

She marveled that she had never before felt so truly alive—so conscious of every bright flower, every sweet-throated bird, every sunbeam that glinted off the rippling water. They laughed over everything and over nothing, and by midday, she admitted to herself, deep down inside, that she'd become infatuated by the stranger from across the Channel, just as the bards had described it in the ancient love poems.

"Brother Francis provided us with a picnic," Ranulf said as he brought Thunder to a stop near yet another stream.

"Brother Francis?" Bridget asked, amazed.

"He's been handling most of the cooking since you left, and complains of it night and day."

She smiled. "Poor Francis. He does better eating food than preparing it. I'll be back to relieve him of his duties soon."

He reached up to help her off the horse's back. "None too soon for him, I'm afraid. But we'll hope he did well enough by us today."

"I'm not even hungry," Bridget said, but when Ranulf pulled a bag from his saddle and produced some chicken and a flask of wine and laid out the repast on a blanket he'd brought along, she found herself enjoying it with as much enthusiasm as he.

"I bought these in town on the way back from the sheriff's this morning," he said, digging into the bag for two fruit tarts like the one she'd enjoyed so much the previous day. The pastries had not held up well on their morning ride. "Blast," he said. "They're ruined."

"Of course, they're not," Bridget said, grabbing the mangled tart from his hand and eagerly biting into it. Ranulf ignored his own tart as he watched Bridget finish hers with great relish. "It's delicious," she said, her mouth full.

He laughed and leaned over to kiss the sticky syrup from the corner of her mouth. "*You're* delicious," he said. She gave a happy giggle and made a motion to clean the excess tart off her face with the back of her hand. "Let me," he said, his voice suddenly altered.

Her laughter died in her throat as he gently nibbled at her lower lip, then broadened his kiss to her entire mouth. "You must eat yours," she murmured.

He threw his tart to one side. "Nay, I'll take the sweeter fruit this day," he said. Then he began to kiss her again. The kisses were tender, at first, as they had been on the previous day, but soon took on a kind of urgency that was new. His mouth and tongue moved over hers like silky fire. She felt a trembling in her middle and a kind of wild rush that radiated upward and downward at the same time from some point deep inside her.

"Ranulf," she whispered. The sound of his own name seemed to ignite him. Without stopping his kisses, he pressed her back on the blanket and moved his hand over her breast. She moaned as she felt her nipple harden under his slow strokes. For a moment, she looked past him to see the cloudless blue sky above them, then she closed her eyes and let herself be drawn into the vortex of sensations being produced by his mouth and his hands.

After several endless moments, he stopped with a groan of frustration, and rolled over to lie beside her. She opened her eyes and turned her head toward him. "Thank you," she whispered.

Ranulf's eyes were closed. He chuckled without opening them. "For giving you your *second* real kiss?"

"Aye. Though 'twas more than one."

"Quite a few more."

"I wasn't counting," she said. "I wouldn't even have objected to more."

"Nay, we stopped just in time."

"In time for what?"

He opened his eyes and boosted himself up on an elbow to look down at her. "In time to save your virtue, sweetheart. I'd not have been responsible for my behavior if we'd continued."

Bridget had a vague notion what he was trying to say, but she considered his worry a bit silly. What need did she have to protect her virtue, especially if she was going to spend the rest of her life in a monastery?

"I wouldn't have objected to a few more, just the same," she said grumpily.

He leaned over to plant a brief kiss on her pouting lips. "Which is why I'm going to take you safely back to the Marchands'," he said firmly, "before those big, velvety brown eyes of yours make me lose my resolve."

Her fantasy day was over. Tomorrow or the next day, Ranulf would ride away on his search for his brother. She would return to her duties at the abbey. Francis could give up his cooking chores, which would no doubt be as much a relief to the other monks as to the portly Francis himself. Everything would return to normal. But she would always have this one perfect day. No one could take that away from her now.

They made good time back to the cottage. As they'd left their picnic site, Bridget had been surprised to see that the sun was already sinking, and she felt a stab of remorse for leaving the Marchands for the entire day. She hoped that Claudine had had no trouble getting the cook fire restarted.

"The Marchands will wonder where we've been all day," she said, as Ranulf helped her down from Thunder.

"Nay, I warrant they won't wonder at all," he said, and grinned.

Bridget smiled briefly. The cottage seemed strangely quiet. There was no light coming from the two small windows, no smell of a fire burning or food cooking. Even the birds seemed to have stopped twittering in the trees.

Her throat closed around a dreadful wave of foreboding. "Claudine!" she called.

Ranulf was adjusting Thunder's bridle and had not appeared to notice anything amiss, but at the tone of her voice, he turned sharply. "Are you all right?" he asked.

Instead of answering, she ran headlong into the cottage. Philip still lay on the bed where she'd left him that morning. Claudine was crumpled in a heap on the floor with the peas Bridget had shelled spilled all about her.

Bridget stumbled backward in horror.

Chapter Eight

Ranulf helped Bridget steady herself and would have held her longer, but she pulled out of his grasp and flew across the room to kneel by Claudine's side.

The old woman was still breathing, and as Bridget lifted her head to cradle it in her lap, Claudine's eyes fluttered open. "Philip," she rasped.

Ranulf had gone to check on the old man and was looking back at Bridget with stricken eyes.

Bridget pulled Claudine more firmly into her arms and rocked her like a babe. She gulped back a sob that threatened to choke her. Had Claudine slipped while trying to prepare the meal Bridget had planned? But what of Philip? There was no sign of blood. Except for the spilled peas, nothing else seemed amiss.

Ranulf lifted Philip into the center of the bed and

straightened his limbs, then pulled a blanket over the top of him. Claudine started to moan as she watched him.

Bridget dropped a kiss on the woman's forehead and asked, "Are you injured? Do you hurt somewhere?"

The old woman shook her head. Tears started falling out of the corner of each eye and rolled down her cheeks onto Bridget's hands.

Ranulf walked over to the two women and knelt beside them. "Can you tell us what happened?" he asked gently. She seemed unable to answer. Ranulf and Bridget exchanged a look of helplessness.

"Do they have any family here in Beauville?" Ranulf asked.

Bridget shook her head. "Only a daughter in Rouen."

He looked for a moment at the older woman, who was still moaning in Bridget's arms. "Do they have some wine here?" he asked.

Bridget pointed to the wooden larder cupboard. He stood and went to retrieve a flask, which he brought back and, kneeling again, held to the old woman's lips.

After a couple of sips, she pushed it away with her hand and motioned that she wanted to get up. It was several more minutes before Ranulf and Bridget were able to get her off the floor and situated on a stool that she insisted be placed directly next to her husband's body. Bridget quickly cleaned up the peas and mopped the spilled water, guilt pounding behind her ears.

"Did you have an accident? Was the pot too heavy to lift?" she asked finally.

The color was returning to Claudine's white face. "Nay, child. 'Twas no accident."

Ranulf put a hand on the woman's shoulder to steady her and said calmly, "Tell us what happened, good mother."

In a halting voice, Claudine told them that she and Philip had been awakened from their nap by armed men. She was unsure of the number.

"The leader was a huge man," she said. "And when my Philip tried to keep him away, he swatted him backward as if he'd been no more than a child. His arms were that powerful, and he wore black wristlets that looked to be made of metal. He knocked my Philip clear across the room. Then he just crumpled there…on the bed."

Ranulf remembered exactly such a wristlet descending toward his own head on the road to St. Gabriel. Hellfire, he berated himself. It hadn't occurred to him that his attackers might still be looking for him to complete the job they started. "Were they asking about me?" he asked the old woman.

She looked up at him, surprised. "About you? Nay, they were asking about Bridget."

The Marchands' neighbors, the Courmiers, had been summoned to help. Pierre, the dairyman they had met in the marketplace, had come with his five brothers and had taken Philip's body to the church to await burial. Claudine had agreed to go to the Courmiers' dairy farm until her daughter could be contacted.

Bridget let the old women go with a last fervent hug. She didn't like to leave her, but she was sick with the knowledge that it had been her presence in the old couple's life that had led to this. Claudine would be safer away from her.

"There were no bruises on the old man's body," Ranulf said after everyone else had left. "His heart probably just gave out with the fright."

"What kind of people would bully an innocent old couple like that?" she asked. "I can't believe there are such fiends in this world."

Ranulf put his arm around her. "Aye, 'tis a sad fact of life. Yet there are many more good people than evil."

Bridget was unconvinced. Her brief time "on the outside" had been much less exhilarating and, at the end, much more horrifying than any of her imaginings over the years. She was ready to retreat behind the familiar and safe walls of St. Gabriel. If they were still safe.

"What if those men, whoever they are, come to the abbey looking for me? Could the monks be in danger, too?"

"You've said that no one ever knew of your presence there. I think it's the perfect place for you until we discover who these men are and what they want."

"And you will be at St. Gabriel, too?"

Ranulf looked around the neat little cottage where all the earthly evidence of the Marchands' life together remained unchanged. "Aye," he said. "Until this riddle is solved, I'll be there, too."

Pierre Courmier had agreed to take good care of Claudine Marchand until her daughter came. They hadn't told him where Bridget intended to go, and he hadn't asked.

Ranulf wanted to question Camille Courmier further about why she had called Bridget by the name Charlotte, but he decided that he should see Bridget safely back to the abbey before he set about making his inquiries.

As soon as the couple returned to St. Gabriel and told their story to Brother Alois, he called a meeting of his counselors and Francis, who was an ex officio member of the panel. They quickly agreed that Bridget should stay hidden at the abbey, and that Ranulf could be allowed to stay while he tried to discover the identity of the assailants, who he felt were the same men who had waylaid him on the road.

It was the last topic of the meeting that led to disagreements.

"She has a right to know her own background," Francis argued. "Especially now, when it looks as if something in that background might be putting her in danger."

"What danger?" Ebert asked. "A confused old woman thought the men were after Bridget. They could as well have been after the knight."

Cyril agreed. "Aye. If no one has come searching for her in all these years she's lived here, why would they suddenly be looking now?"

"I think we should open Abbot Josef's records and find out the truth," Francis said firmly. "Or do you already know the answer, Brother Alois?"

All three monks looked at the abbot. "What I know is that Bridget was given to us as a sacred trust. We gave her the name of a virginal saint and raised her to be pure so that she could overcome the sin of her unholy birth."

Francis snorted. "Bridget had nothing to do with her birth, and she has no sin to overcome. She's pure of heart, which is the important thing."

Brother Ebert stood and started to pace the length of the sacristy. "No one's arguing Bridget's good heart, Brother Francis. The problem is what do we do about her? If 'tis true that people are looking for her, then it's possible they could find her here."

Cyril nodded reluctantly. "It might be time to consider another place where she could live safely. We don't want people prying into abbey affairs. We've our inventions to consider."

Francis shook his head. "I don't care about the inventions, only about Bridget. If this is the safest place for her, then we should keep her here. But I think for everyone's safety, we should open Abbot Josef's records and find out who her mother really was."

Brother Alois's head was down and he appeared lost in deep thought. "Abbot Josef's last words to me were that because of her parentage, the abbey of St. Gabriel would keep Bridget forever in its care."

"Aye, but that's because of Brother Ren—" Francis began.

Alois raised his hand to interrupt him. None of the monks were ever allowed to speak the name of the monk whose sin of the flesh had led to Bridget's birth.

"'Tis because it's our sacred charge, Francis," Alois said calmly. "And that's all we need know about it. Bridget will stay here at St. Gabriel. And Abbot Josef's book will stay sealed.''

Cyril and Ebert exchanged a frustrated glance, but Alois's demeanor clearly indicated that the discussion was over.

Bridget was unaware that her fate was being decided by the abbey council. She was back home again, inside the four walls of her tiny house in the old brewery. It felt comfortable and *safe*. She should never have left, she told herself over and over as she put on her nightdress to sleep. She should have held firm and stayed at the abbey.

If she'd never left St. Gabriel, she would have missed the chance to see the marketplace at Beauville and ride Thunder through springtime meadows. She would have missed knowing Ranulf's kisses. But if she'd stayed home, Philip and Claudine Marchand would this very moment be falling into a peaceful sleep in each other's arms.

She jumped at the sound of a knock on her door. It was an unaccustomed sound, since the monks never sought her here in her private sanctuary. The visitor could be only one person, and she felt her pulse surge, in spite of herself.

Ranulf's face showed the strain of the long day and made her remember that only a short time ago she had thought he had little chance to live. ''I came to see if you're all right,'' he said, his voice weary.

She held the door barely ajar, but when she noticed a slight sway to his stance, she opened it more widely to admit him. "Sit on the bed," she told him. "I should take a look at your wound."

"I wanted to check your condition, not the other way around," he protested, but he did as she told him. She took a seat beside him.

The bandage had not been changed for some time and came off with difficulty. He winced as it pulled on a raw spot. "You should really have another poultice," she told him. She was careful to keep her voice detached. Her fantasy day with Ranulf was over.

He looked a little surprised at her tone, but excused it with the observation, "It's not been an easy day for you."

"Nay. Nor for you. This is seeping again, and if you don't take care of it properly, you'll have the poisons back." This time her voice was almost angry, and as she stood to fetch her medical supplies, he grabbed her hand and pulled her back.

"Is there something else the matter, angel? Besides the Marchands?"

She pulled her hand away and walked over to the chest where she kept her box of supplies. Couldn't he see that *everything* was the matter?

Couldn't he see that after his kisses of this afternoon, she would never, ever be the same? And that all she wanted was to be the same and to have her secret life a secret again so that no one else would be in jeopardy because of her? "A man is dead because of me," she said coldly. "Don't you think that's enough reason to be upset?"

He studied her across the room for a long moment, then answered quietly, "Of course it is."

Neither said a word for several moments while she dressed his wound with fresh salve and a clean bandage. "That's better," she said finally.

"I thank you," he said, standing. "I'll let you sleep now."

She stood back to allow him to leave, avoiding his gaze. "Good night." Her voice was stiff.

He reached for her hands, but she held them firmly clasped in front of her. Finally he took her chin in his hand to force her to look at him. "Bridget, we will find those men. They will pay for what they've done."

"With more violence?" she asked. "With more people suffering for my cause? When I don't even know what my cause is?"

"You need to let me help you."

She just looked down at the floor, shaking her head.

After a moment, he said, "You're tired. We'll

talk more in the morning when we've both had some sleep.'' He waited for her to speak, and when she still remained silent, he said softly, ''Good night, angel.'' Then he turned and left the room.

Bridget doused the candle and slipped into her bed. Her throat burned with unshed tears, but the tears only added to the weight of her guilt. She should be crying for Philip and Claudine and their lost love, but deep down she knew that instead she was crying for herself and for the love she would never have a chance to know.

Charles Guise had waited for several hours in the baron's antechamber at Darmaux Castle, but did nothing to reveal his impatience as he was finally ushered into LeClerc's study. It was past midnight.

''What did you find out?'' LeClerc snapped.

Guise gave his customary bow. ''The old man's body is at the church. They're to bury him first thing in the morning. There'll be no questions.''

LeClerc nodded. ''The old woman lives?''

''Aye. But she's to be shipped off to a daughter's home in Rouen. She'll bring us no trouble.''

''Good. Did you find out why the girl was staying there?''

''Just the same information we had before—that she was living with the Marchands and that she was in Beauville yesterday with the English knight. Now she seems to have vanished.''

The baron had arrived at the sheriff's house that morning well before dawn, but he showed no sign of tiredness. He stood up and walked around the table to where the sheriff stood before him. ''People do not vanish, Guise. Has she gone back to the abbey?''

''I don't know, milord.''

The baron's eyes glittered in the light of the dozen or more wall sconces that lined his study. ''So,'' he said softly, ''why are you standing here instead of going to find out?''

''You sent for me, milord,'' Guise answered calmly.

''I sent for you to bring me answers. You have not done so.''

''I thought you—''

LeClerc swiped the back of his hand across the sheriff's face. ''You are not in my employ to think. Now go find out where she went.''

''On the morrow—''

''Not tomorrow, tonight. If our contact at St. Gabriel has betrayed us, I want to know about it now.''

''Aye, milord,'' the sheriff said, his head down.

''What are you waiting for?'' the baron shouted.

Guise bowed and backed out of the room, waiting until he had closed the door behind him before he lifted a hand to rub his reddened cheek.

It felt good to be back in her own kitchen. Bridget had been up before dawn and had skipped morning prayers to go directly to the kitchen to have fresh bread ready for the monks to break their morning fast. She'd also made a quick weeding pass at the vegetable garden, checked the monks' beds in the dormitory, remaking several of them, scrubbed the tables and the wooden floor of the refectory, hauled several pails of water from the well, and plucked and dressed five chickens for dinner.

By late morning, she was sweaty and red faced. Her hair had pulled out of its net snood to fly every which way. She'd eaten nothing, and her hands trembled as she seated herself next to the kitchen fireplace and took a piece of bread out of Ebert's bread-slicing machine.

"I'd heard rumors of a divine whirlwind making its way through the abbey this morning." Francis squeezed his way through the narrow kitchen door. "Turns out it was just our little Bridget come back to us."

Bridget gave a wan smile. "My adventure on the outside did not go as planned, Francis, and I fear 'twas chiefly my fault."

The monk pulled a stool to sit opposite her. "You can't blame yourself for the evil that exists in the world, child."

She shook her head. "Those men would not have known to come looking for me if I hadn't gone out into town with Sir Ranulf. It was nothing more than my own willfulness and wicked curiosity that caused poor Philip's death."

"There's nothing wicked about curiosity. Bridget, you've spent your entire lifetime shut away in this place. It would be unnatural if you *didn't* wonder what the rest of the world was like."

"From now on I'll let my curiosity be satisfied in the abbey library. I'm pleased to be back."

Francis looked at the slice of bread she held clenched in her hand, uneaten. "So pleased that you plan to work and starve yourself into exhaustion? You've not eaten anything since you arrived."

Bridget glanced down at the bread in surprise. "I was eating." She then amended, "I was just about to."

"Mmm-hmm." Francis bent over, puffing, picked up a cup from beside the hearth and dipped it into the kettle of soup that sat at the edge of the fire. Then he held it out to her. "Aye, you're about to while I sit here and watch you. Don't say another word until you drink this."

Bridget was not sure her stomach would welcome the attention, but she did as the monk asked, and had to admit that after she finished the soup, she felt better.

"There," Francis said with a satisfied clap of his hands. "A body without food is like a soul without prayer—it's unnatural."

Francis had never been one to stint on either account, Bridget thought with a sudden wave of affection. She could see worry in his kind eyes. "I'll be all right, Francis," she said softly.

"Aye, lass, I know you will. But you mustn't be afraid to admit the things that are changing in your life."

Bridget stared into the fire. "Nothing needs to change. I'm back where I belong."

Francis leaned forward and regarded her with a shrewd gaze. "And do you think you will still be satisfied with your life here?"

She looked up at him. "I was only gone for two days, Brother Francis. It's hardly time for me to have changed that much."

"I wasn't only thinking about your stay in town."

Of all the monks, Francis had always been the one who had been able to see into her heart. He was the one she had run to for comfort through the minor trials of childhood. Though their roles had changed over the years as she began to assume more and more duties at the abbey, he still was the closest thing to a father she had. And he was a wise man.

"You mean Ranulf," she said slowly.

He nodded. "I could see it in your face when he brought you back here yesterday. I think you've fallen in love with him."

Bridget gave her shoulders a little shake. "Nay, not love. We've had only a little time together."

"But you wish it could be more?"

"'Tis foolish to wish for things that cannot be. Ranulf is a noble from a great estate in England. Soon he'll be gone from here and from my life. And the sooner the better, I'd say, for look at the chain of troubles his arrival set in motion."

Francis seemed to be reflecting for a moment. Finally he said, "Perhaps his arrival was divine providence, Bridget—a message to all of us that we cannot expect to keep you here forever."

But Bridget would hear nothing of his arguments. She'd had her first true kiss and many more after that. She'd felt the tingle on her skin and the racing of her heart. She'd never forget it, but now it was time for her to retreat into the netherworld that had been her home since birth—before anyone else she cared about got hurt.

Chapter Nine

Finally it appeared that he was going to be able to question the sheriff of Beauville. There were a number of horses tied in front of the sheriff's house as Ranulf rode up on Thunder after stopping at the blacksmith's to pick up his arms. He slowed to a halt, then dismounted and began tying Thunder at the gate as a guard emerged and came down the path toward him.

"State your business," the man said.

It seemed an unfriendly welcome for a provincial sheriff, but Ranulf reminded himself that there'd been a violent death in the town the previous day. "My business is with the sheriff," he told the man pleasantly. "I've some questions to ask him about a missing person."

The man eyed Ranulf's strange attire. He still wore the pig farmer's humble tunic and boots, yet over it he had placed a tooled belt containing the smith's finest dagger, and on his head he wore a small leather helmet that covered his head bandage. "You may give me your name and I'll let the sheriff know you're here."

Ranulf told the guard his name and waited patiently while the man disappeared inside the sheriff's house, which, unlike the surrounding cottages, was built of a sturdy brick. It was several minutes before the man reappeared and motioned him to enter.

Charles Guise was seated in the far corner of the room in a deep master's chair with arms that gave it the look of a throne. He didn't stand or make any acknowledgment at the knight's entrance, but Ranulf ignored the insult. He was here to get information, not exchange courtesies.

"We have no idea why my brother would have been wanting to find St. Gabriel," Ranulf explained at the conclusion of his story. "And no one at the abbey seems to have heard anything of him."

Guise's only response to his account was a question. "You have been staying at the abbey, then?"

"Aye. They cared for me after the incident on the highway."

"You were lucky that they found you." There was a curious detachment to the sheriff's observation.

"But not so lucky to have been waylaid in the first place, wouldn't you agree?" Ranulf asked dryly.

"Perhaps you should take it as a sign that the Crusades are over. It's time for English knights to return to their homelands and leave us in peace."

At Lyonsbridge Ranulf had been raised with a respect for authority and the rule of law. He had not expected to be mistrustful of the sheriff. But the longer they talked, the more he began to dislike the man. Nevertheless, he kept his tone civil as he said, "I'll be happy to return to England as soon as my brother can ride home at my side. I was hoping that you might be able to help me with my search, but if you have no information, I'll begin my own inquiries."

"Have you found out anything that would explain your brother's interest in St. Gabriel?"

"Nay. I've questioned the monks there. They can make no sense of it."

Guise remained silent for a long moment, then leaned forward and said, "After all this time, your brother has no doubt met the same fate as thousands of other mercenaries just like him. A fate which could be yours as well if you persist in staying where you're not welcome."

The sheriff then stood and walked out of the shadowy corner toward Ranulf. For the first time,

Ranulf was able to get a clear look at the man. He was a big man, dressed in a long-sleeved shirt under a heavy tunic. On each arm he wore a long wristlet forged of black metal.

Ranulf drew in a sharp breath, but Guise didn't seem to notice. The sheriff now stood directly in front of him. Two of the sheriff's men were in the room, as well, and the atmosphere had suddenly become menacing. He had not gotten a clear look at the men who had attacked him, but he'd never forget those massive arms in their black wristlets.

"I'm sorry you are unable to help me in my quest, Sheriff," Ranulf said smoothly as he quickly assessed the situation. "I trust you serve the people of Beauville better than you do its visitors."

He knew there was at least one other guard outside the sheriff's house. With the sheriff, that made four armed men against one armed only with a knife. His only advantage was that the sheriff was unaware of Ranulf's suspicions.

"We have no use for strangers in this part of Normandy," Guise said with a sneer. Both of the sheriff's men had straightened up, tensing for action.

In a move he had learned in the Saracen campaign, Ranulf turned slightly and gave a sideways kick into Guise's midsection. The big man made a sound like "ooph" and crumpled backward, a star-

tled expression on his face. Before his astonished
guards could move, Ranulf took a running dive out
the window, losing his new helmet and scraping
his head along the brick as he rolled head over
heels onto the ground outside.

The fourth guard outside jumped at the sudden
commotion, but Ranulf was halfway down the path
by the time he had risen to his feet. In the few
seconds it took the guard to retrieve his sword and
follow, Ranulf had leaped onto Thunder's back and
was galloping away.

Blood streamed into his eyes as he rode, and he
realized that his window acrobatics had torn open
his head wound and had, perhaps, deepened it. He
muttered a curse at his own carelessness. He hadn't
originally thought about danger when he set out to
find Dragon, but the attack on the road should have
warned him.

Now he was in a dilemma. He had no idea why
the sheriff of Beauville wanted him dead, but he
evidently did. And Ranulf had had ample opportunity to see that these were dangerous men. The
last thing he wanted to do was to lead them into
the peaceful life of the abbey, especially since he
knew that Bridget was there.

He could ride away from Beauville and head
back home where he could nurse his wound until

he was better and then return with reinforcements from Lyonsbridge.

But the men at the Marchand household had been searching for Bridget not Ranulf, though the logical conclusion was that those men and his at-tackers were one and the same. Now that the sheriff knew that he'd been staying at the abbey, he would undoubtedly go there looking for him. Before any other course of action, he had to reach Bridget and be sure she was safe.

He reached the fork in the road and pulled left on Thunder's reins to steer the big animal in the direction of St. Gabriel.

"I mislike the idea of storming into the abbey to get him, if indeed he was fool enough to go back there," Henri LeClerc said more to himself than to the sheriff, who had spent the past half hour on his knees at LeClerc's feet.

"My men would take care not to harm the op-erations of the furnace," Guise said. "I could arrest him for assaulting me and take him well away from the monastery before we deal with him. The monks never need to know what happens to him."

LeClerc remained silent, scowling. Finally he said, "This is turning out to be a bigger problem than I had anticipated. We thought he was merely a nosy knight who had gotten wind of St. Gabriel's discovery. But now that we know he's from an estate as powerful as Lyonsbridge, I'm not sure if killing him will solve our problem. They'll only send more in his wake.''

''What do you want to do?'' Guise made no indication that his knees had begun to ache. He knew that he was lucky that the baron hadn't ordered him decapitated on the spot when he had had to tell him that he'd had Ranulf inside his own house and let the knight escape.

The baron began pacing the length of his study. ''If he stays at the abbey, we'll leave him alone. Eventually he'll become convinced that no one knows anything about his brother and he'll return home.''

The sheriff did not look pleased at the baron's decision, but he held his tongue. ''So you want me to keep my men away from the abbey?''

''For the time being.''

''What about the girl? Our informant says she's back at the abbey.''

LeClerc considered the matter a moment. ''If she stays hidden there, we'll let the matter ride for the moment. There will be plenty of time to get rid of her after the weapons are finished and on their way to the duke.''

''Shall I tell the monk that we're holding off for the time being?''

"Nay, let the damned cleric sweat a little over our next move. When the weapons are done, I think it will be time to deal with him, as well. There will be no need to keep the secrets of St. Gabriel once the world knows of them."

"Aye, milord."

LeClerc motioned that the sheriff could rise and leave. Guise stood and rubbed his cramped legs. As he bowed and backed toward the door, the baron stopped him. "One more thing, Guise."

"Aye, milord?"

"'Tis time we disposed of our prisoner in Mordin Castle."

"I thought that once the weapons are finished you were going to offer him to the duke to hold for ransom."

LeClerc dropped heavily into his chair. "Aye, but I've changed my mind. With Lyonsbridge sending men to look for him, we can't risk holding him. There's too much else at stake. Get rid of him."

"Aye, milord," Guise said with another bow. Then he backed out of the room.

The dizziness started about halfway back to St. Gabriel, and by the time he was within sight of the abbey, Ranulf had all he could do to keep himself up on his horse. Fortunately, Thunder needed little guidance and kept a steady pace toward the cluster of fieldstone buildings.

He couldn't remember reaching them. The next thing he knew, he was once again in his small cell, once again with his head throbbing in great waves of pain, and once again looking up into the tawny round eyes of his very own angel.

"What happened?" he asked.

She smiled. "That was going to be my question to you. I was going to ask it after I'd finished scolding you for ruining all my good nursing."

He closed his eyes a moment, hoping that the room would be steadier when he opened them again. It wasn't. "I'm sorry to be such a bad patient."

Her smile died as he grimaced at a stab of pain. "You've opened the wound again," she told him unnecessarily.

"It feels as if I've opened my entire head."

"Nay, there's still some left to crack if you want to go out and bash it yet one more time."

He could tell that her sharp tone masked concern. "Not today," he rasped.

"I should say not today, Sir Knight, for I don't intend to let you up from this bed for the next week. I'll call the monks to restrain you, if I must."

In good health, Ranulf could probably have mastered the forty monks of St. Gabriel single-

handedly, but at the moment he felt weak as a new-
born kitten. He wanted nothing more than to float
back into some kind of dream world where his head
was detached from his body. But he hadn't come
to St. Gabriel to rest.

"I can't stay here, angel. Nor can you. It's not
safe."

"Did you find out something about the men who
were looking for me at the Marchands'?"

"Aye, I believe the men who were looking for
you were led by none other than the sheriff of
Beauville himself."

"The sheriff!"

Ranulf struggled to sit up, but Bridget pushed
him down again. "I have to get you away before
they come here looking for me," he said.

She pressed firmly on his shoulders. "The devil
himself may come after you, Ranulf, but you're not
getting up. You lost so much blood on your way
in here that it's a wonder you have a drop left in
you. You're not moving."

It didn't take her hold on his shoulders to tell
him that he was weak. He could scarcely move.
"Then call Francis and the abbot," he told her. "I
need to talk with them."

He drifted to sleep while she went to fetch the
two monks, but struggled to open his eyes when
they appeared beside his bed with Brother Ebert

and Prior Cyril behind them. "You might have to be ready for a visit from the sheriff and his men," he told them.

Brother Alois looked concerned but said calmly, "They are welcome here, as are any of the good Christians of Beauville."

"I don't know if the sheriff is a good Christian, Brother, but he's a darn good fighter. He's the one who split my head open like a ripe plum."

"Sheriff Guise?" Alois repeated. "Surely, you're mistaken, my son."

The other three monks looked skeptical. Ranulf wished his head would stop pounding for just a moment, long enough to allow him to make a coherent argument. "You must take my word for it. What's more, I believe it was the sheriff and his men who raided the Marchand house in search of Bridget."

"We should never have let her outside the walls," Cyril said. "She was perfectly safe here until you offered shelter to this stranger. Nothing's been right since then."

Bridget turned her head sharply toward Cyril. The monk sounded genuinely upset about the possible danger to her, and she was surprised. Cyril rarely talked of anything but scientific theories and the latest goings-on behind the walls of the work shed. She was touched by his concern.

Alois said to Ranulf, "I believe Bridget is right that you're in no condition to be moved. We'll keep a watch out on the road for intruders and if anyone comes, we'll be sure that Bridget is safely hidden away."

"We might be able to come up with a few tricks of our own to scare them off," Ebert said, rubbing his hands together. Bridget recognized the gleam that he got in his eye each time he was on the verge of a new invention.

"Let's just hope that Sir Ranulf is wrong about the sheriff," she said. "What we'd all like is for St. Gabriel to settle back into its normal routine."

With nods of agreement, the four monks filed out of the room, leaving Bridget alone with Ranulf, whose eyes were again closed.

She put her hand gently over his new bandage to check if the wound was abnormally warm. Then she pulled the blanket up around him and started to turn around to leave.

"Will they truly post a guard?" he asked weakly.

"Let's call it a *watch*," she replied. "But, aye, Alois always does what he says he will do."

"Tomorrow, I'll take you away from here." His speech was slurred. "To Lyonsbridge. Safe there."

Bridget smiled sadly. "Aye, tomorrow," she agreed. Lyonsbridge. The place had a magnificent sound, but it wasn't a place she would likely see tomorrow or any other day. She stood watching him a long moment as his breathing evened out into sleep. Then, instead of leaving, she fetched a stool from the hall and sat down next to his bed.

Ranulf awoke slowly. He'd dreamed that he was back at Lyonsbridge, engaged in one of his accustomed wrestling matches with Dragon. His brother had taken a hold on Ranulf's head and refused to let go, even though the usually friendly game had become too serious. As the room came into focus, he realized that the head pain had not come from Edmund, but from his wound. His mouth was dry as dust.

He was alone in the dim cell, and no candle burned on the stand at his side. Where was she? he thought in sudden panic. Had the sheriff's men come to the abbey and found her while he'd been dead to the world? He sat bolt upright in the bed as pain splintered through his temple.

"What do you think you're doing, Ranulf Brand?" came her indignant voice from the doorway.

With a sigh of relief, he sank back against the mattress. "I didn't know where you were," he mumbled, feeling grumpy and sore.

Bridget sailed into the room and set the tray she

was carrying down on the floor. "I do have a few other duties around here beside you," she said. "How are you feeling this morning?"

"Morning?" He looked sideways toward the window. The nondescript patch of gray sky that was visible gave no hint of the hour.

"Well, almost midday. You've slept the day around and then some."

"And nothing's happened? The sheriff's men haven't come looking for either one of us?"

"It's been peaceful as a lullaby. Unless you count Ebert's fit over Cyril using pieces of his water clock to repair his blast fire."

"What's a blast fire?" Ranulf asked the question absently. His mind was more intent on the proprietary note in Bridget's voice when she talked about *her* monks.

"A blast fire is…I'm not sure, exactly. But the monks are dreadfully proud of it. It's out in the work shed with most of their other tinkerings."

"I'd like to see it."

"I'm sure they'd be happy to show you. They're proud of their inventions, even though 'tis a sin according to the Rule."

"Inventions?"

"No, pride," Bridget explained with a little grin. Ranulf sat up again, more carefully this time.

"Did Abbot Alois put up the guard he promised against any unwanted visitors?"

"Guards aren't necessary. We see any visitors coming when they're half a league away since the only road is across the meadow. There hasn't been so much as a rabbit on it since you rode back from town." Her eyes took on that merry gleam he had come to recognize. "It could be that the sheriff's men would rather wait until you leave the abbey again rather than face the fearsome White Monks of St. Gabriel."

"Fearsome? Ebert's a tall fellow, grant you. But Francis has the speed of a tortoise and Alois is getting on in years—"

She interrupted him. "'Tis not their strength that scares folks, 'tis their eccentricities. You never know around here when you're going to be caught up in one of their harebrained projects. I remember when the blacksmith came last month to repair the iron railing around the bell tower, Ebert and Cyril had him trapped up on top of the tower for half the afternoon while they tried to perfect a new relay system they'd invented." The words were rich with affection.

"But you love them," Ranulf said softly.

"Aye. They are my fathers. Every one of them."

He shook his head. "I've never heard the like.

It's hard to believe that they've been able to keep you secret here all these years.''

''As I said before, this is a quiet place. The people of Beauville mostly leave us to our own devices.''

''What about the church officials? Do they know you live here?''

''Gracious, no! That's why we've had to be so careful. It would be the end of St. Gabriel if it were ever discovered.'' Her expression changed from happy to alarmed. ''You must never tell anyone.''

''I won't reveal your secret, angel,'' he said. ''But I still think 'tis no kind of place for a beautiful young woman. Think of all of life you are missing.''

She looked wistful for only a moment before she smiled and said, ''But I didn't miss out on my first kiss, did I? Nor on the second, if you recall.''

Ranulf groaned. ''Aye, I recall very well, minx.'' He swung his legs down from the bed, but had no strength left to attempt to stand. His gut ached with wanting to kiss her again, but instead he said softly, ''Nor am I likely to forget.''

She was quiet for a long moment as their gazes held. Then she cleared her throat and said briskly, ''You're still weak. You need some food in you.'' She pointed to the tray. ''Can you eat that by yourself?''

He nodded. He'd be able to eat well enough once his insides stopped churning. "Aye, go ahead and be about your duties. I'll be fine."

She hesitated a moment longer, then picked up the tray and put it beside him on the bed. "Start with the soup, nice and slow," she ordered. Her chatelaine voice was back. He might as well be one of her charges.

"Yes, mistress," he said with a grin.

She nodded, waited until he had picked up the spoon, then left.

By afternoon he was feeling as fit as he had before he'd visited the sheriff's house, and he felt a little silly lying in bed like an invalid. Bridget had brought him another set of clothes. They were as plain as the pig farmer's had been, but smelled of soap and sunshine.

He slipped them on and left the building. The day was still gloomy. Heavy, dark clouds hung in the sky to the west and there was a feeling of dampness to the air.

The dormitory had been empty, which meant that the monks should be about their daily duties, but the courtyard looked deserted. He could see no one in the garden or working around the barn.

Suddenly he heard the hollow bong of the church bell and realized that it was the hour of afternoon prayers, which explained the empty complex. He supposed it would be proper to go join them, but now that he had left his bed and his stuffy room, he had no desire to spend the next hour inside on his knees.

Scanning the horizon, he studied the road leading into the abbey and saw that Bridget had spoken the truth. There was no cover leading up to the abbey gate. They would see intruders from quite a distance.

But, in spite of Bridget's defense of her monks, he couldn't imagine that he alone and the monks of St. Gabriel would be a match for trained warriors. He should leave this place now and return to Lyonsbridge for reinforcements. And he should take Bridget with him.

He started walking in the direction of the kitchen, though he assumed that Bridget was at prayers, as well. Then he saw her, racing out of the barn and toward the church, her skirts hiked up in her hands and her hair flying out loose behind her.

As she rounded the corner of the kitchen, she caught sight of him and stopped. Dropping her skirts and pushing back her hair, she continued walking at a more dignified pace, but this time in his direction.

"How are you feeling?" she asked.

"Better. Good, in fact. I've been abed enough for one day."

"Are you on your way to prayers?"

"Not if I can think of an alternative," he said with a grimace.

She laughed. "I often try to think up excuses for my own absences."

"You could say that you were tending to me," he suggested.

"Do you need tending?"

The hint of flirtation to her tone belied the fact that she had spent her life in a monastery. It made his pulse race. "I could," he said, "if it would absolve us both of an hour of prayers."

They exchanged a mutual grin. "You said you wanted to see the monks' tinkerings. This would be a good time to show you the work shed, while they're all in church."

He'd forgotten about wanting to see the inventions, but as he stood near her, smelling the lavender of her hair and listening to the sweet sound of her voice, he'd follow her anywhere she wanted to take him. "The work shed, it is," he said.

She let him take her hand as they crossed the compound, tiptoeing like naughty children along the edge of the church where they could hear the muted sounds of the vespers within, and started down the path to the shed. When they reached the clearing in front of the big building, Bridget stopped. "This is it. If the monks are inside working, you hear their clattering all the way back to the abbey compound." They heard no clattering, but there was a curious roaring sound from within the building. "That's the blast fire," Bridget explained.

Ranulf helped her pull open the double doors and they went inside. To the left of the door was a jumbled mass of wooden troughs and little cups. "Oh dear," Bridget said with a rueful glance at the mess. "No wonder Ebert was so upset. That is the remains of his water clock."

Ranulf looked around the shed in wonder. It was full of odd contraptions made up of all variety of wheels and pulleys and levers. "What *is* all this?" he asked.

Bridget sighed. "It's hard to keep track since they seem to change every week, sometimes every day." She pointed to a tall structure in the corner built of narrow wooden timbers. "That's a collapsible ladder," she said. "Brother Jacques built it to take to the orchard for apple picking. Unfortunately, last time they used it, it collapsed on top of Brother Robert and nearly broke his leg. I believe they've brought it back for some readjustments."

"I should think so," Ranulf said with a laugh.

They walked slowly among the various contrivances in the direction of the roaring sound at the far end, which was obviously coming from a huge cylinder that went from a big iron base on the floor and reached up all the way through the roof of the building.

"Here's the blast fire," Bridget told him.

He could feel the heat from yards away. "What's it for?" he asked.

Bridget held the palms of her hands out to the warmth. "The monks say it gets hotter than a regular fire because of the shape and the height."

Ranulf walked toward the big device, looking it up and down. He'd never seen anything quite like it. From inside he could hear the roar of the flames. It sounded like a fire magnified by ten. "It's amazing," he said slowly.

"This is the monks' prize," she said. "They're always talking about it." She pointed to a door cut in the metal. "Once Francis tried to fast-roast a chicken inside. There was nothing left of it but cinders."

Ranulf didn't join in her laugh. "Such a furnace could be capable of incredible things."

"Aye, 'tis what the monks say."

At the far base a series of pipes extended from the furnace and ended at another device that looked like an oversize iron pot. "What's that?" he asked.

"One of Brother Cyril's refinements," she said. "He designed it as an auxiliary furnace to give an extra boost of air just when the fire was at its hottest. But they decided not to use it."

"Why not?"

Bridget shook her head. "He tested it on a model and it blew the whole thing up. Anyway, Brother Cyril says it's plenty hot enough as is."

Ranulf's expression was thoughtful. Most of the brothers' "tinkerings" appeared to be innocent contraptions to ease their life around the abbey, but this was something different. "I wager there would be powerful men around the continent who would like to see this thing in action," he said.

Bridget shrugged. "We don't really get visitors here."

Ranulf's gaze was on a heap of metal that lay scattered to one side of the blast fire. He walked over and picked a piece off the top. "That's the metal they forge," Bridget said.

He looked down at the cold steel in his hands. It was black as coal and hard as a diamond. He'd seen that metal before, he thought to himself. In Jean the Smithy's shop. And on the wrists of the sheriff just before the man's mace had nearly split his skull in two.

Chapter Ten

It appeared that Bridget was not the only secret the monks of St. Gabriel had been harboring all these years, Ranulf thought, his mind still on the amazing blast fire as he rode in the direction of Beauville.

He'd already seen the black metal in action. He remembered the smithy's brawny arm smashing the helmet down with no effect.

But the question that pounded in his mind was: is the black metal what Dragon had been seeking at St. Gabriel? If so, what had happened to him?

He slowed Thunder to a cautious pace as he approached the town. He had no idea why the sheriff and his men hadn't followed him to the abbey, but he was not anxious to encounter any of them by surprise. He veered off the road before he entered the main part of town and made his way by a back route to the smithy's stables at the western edge.

There was no sign of other visitors, and from the inside he could hear the ringing of an anvil.

Tying Thunder to a post, he went quietly up to the stable doors. The blacksmith was alone inside, pounding on a piece of harness. He stopped when he saw Ranulf.

"Good day to you, Sir Ranulf," he said. His tone seemed a little hesitant.

Ranulf walked toward him.

"I trust your purchases were satisfactory," the smithy added.

"Aye. I've come on another matter." He glanced at the shelf where the black helmet had been on his last visit. "I want to ask you about the black helmet you showed me."

Jean laid his hammer to one side and dusted off his large hands. "What about it?" he asked, too casually.

"Where did you get it?"

"It was made at a forge near here."

"At St. Gabriel?"

"How do you know about St. Gabriel?" the smithy asked, surprised.

"I've been staying there with the monks."

Jean looked confused. "Have you come to be a monk or something?"

Ranulf gave a little smile at the idea. "Nay, 'tis not a life for me. I met with an...*accident*, and the monks have been caring for me. I saw their blast fire and remembered the helmet you showed me.''

''They've told me not to speak of it.''

''Who told you?''

The smithy hesitated, then said, ''Sir Ranulf, let me give you some advice. The men who are interested in the black metal want it for themselves and want it badly. They won't take kindly to a stranger asking questions about it.''

Ranulf had been looking around the stable for anything else that appeared to be made of the metal, but could see none. ''I have a reason for needing to know.''

Jean spoke firmly. ''I warrant I'd better have the reason, then, for telling you any more than I have puts me at some risk.''

Ranulf gave a terse account of his search for his brother. He did not color his words with feelings, but he could see a gleam of sympathy in the smithy's eyes.

''He's your little brother, this Dragon?'' Jean asked.

''Aye, by but a year.''

Jean hesitated just a moment, then he stepped around Ranulf and crossed a couple of empty animal stalls to reach a huge chest that sat against the far wall. Throwing open the top, he gestured to the contents and said, ''Here's your black metal, Englishman. Spear points and arrowheads for the army of the Duke of Austria, being supplied to him by his faithful follower, Henri LeClerc, the Baron of Darmaux.''

Ranulf followed him across the room and looked inside. A shaft of sunlight from the open stable roof glinted off the shiny black points. ''Why spear points?'' he asked.

''For one simple reason,'' the smith answered. ''They pierce armor.''

Ranulf gave a low whistle. ''They're that hard?''

''Aye. We've experimented with forging armor and other items, like the helmet I showed you, but 'tis difficult and the steel is so hard that it becomes brittle. But it's perfect for this.'' He gestured once again at the chest.

''Arrows and lances that pierce armor could change the entire nature of warfare.''

''Aye, or win battles for the army that possesses them.'' He reached into the chest and pulled out a four-inch-long spear point. ''With the right blow, this will go through a man's breastplate as if it were butter.''

A sick feeling settled into the pit of Ranulf's stomach. ''Do you make them here?'' Ranulf asked.

''I do some finishing here. They forge them at the abbey.''

"They forge *weapons* at the abbey?"

"Aye."

He stood for a minute in stunned silence. He couldn't believe that the kind, eccentric, absent-minded monks of St. Gabriel were engaged in making weapons of war for an unscrupulous baron and his liege lord, the Duke of Austria. "How many people here in town know about this?" Ranulf asked softly.

"Not many. As I told you, 'tis worth one's life to speak of it."

"But they had to tell you because they needed your skills."

"Aye," said Jean. "The baron needed my skills."

Ranulf looked up in surprise at the sudden venom in the smithy's tone. Carefully he asked, "Do I sense that you are not fond of the baron?"

The smith's knuckles grew white around the spear point he held. "The baron needs me because the other blacksmith in Beauville is dead."

Ranulf tensed. "What happened to him?"

"He was too talkative for the baron's taste."

Once again the two men's gazes met, and this time there was a bolt of understanding exchanged between them. "Was he a good friend of yours?" Ranulf asked gently.

Jean sent the spear point smashing into the chest.

Then he looked up again with hollow eyes and answered, "He was my brother."

"I just want to know," Bridget said firmly. "Ever since I can remember, no one would speak to me of how I got here or where I came from. I didn't hatch from an egg. Somebody here must have some information about me."

She and Francis were scrubbing the long wooden refectory tables with sand. The monk continued his methodical rubbing and avoided looking at her. "I told you, Bridget, that I was afraid the time would come when you would no longer be happy here at the abbey."

Bridget gave her foot a little stomp. "I *am* happy. But I'm also curious. Francis, when I went into Beauville with Ranulf, people stared at me as though I were someone come back from the dead. What do they know? Who did they think I was?"

"Sometimes curiosity is dangerous, child" was all Francis would say.

Bridget wrinkled her nose with frustration. "If you won't tell me, perhaps I'll just have to go back into town and start asking myself."

At this, the monk straightened up, put aside his rag and turned to her. "You mustn't do that, especially now. Think about those men who came looking for you at the Marchands'."

"But don't you see, Brother? That's why I must find out. This is not simply idle curiosity. Why were those men looking for me? Since no one in town has ever seen me before this week, it must be something to do with my past."

Francis hesitated, then pulled out a bench from under the table they'd been cleaning and motioned for her to sit down on one end. When she did so, he settled himself opposite her. "I'll tell you what I can, Bridget."

Bridget's palms started to sweat. In the past, she'd always let herself be dissuaded from asking questions, but this time she was determined to find answers. She braced herself on the bench as though ready for a blow.

"You were born here," he began.

Bridget's eyes widened. "Here? At the abbey?"

"Aye."

"But why—"

Francis held up a hand to interrupt her. "Abbot Josef and Brother Eustacio helped your mother give you birth."

Both monks were now dead. "Did my—my mother have no other family to help her? No women? My father?"

"She had no one but us."

The back of Bridget's throat had gone dry and she rasped as she asked, "What happened to her?"

Francis leaned forward and put his hand over Bridget's where she had it braced on the bench. "She died, child. Twelve days after she gave you life, she lost her own."

Bridget closed her eyes. Twelve days. She'd had a mother for twelve days. "'Twas the birth that killed her?" she asked in a voice barely above a whisper.

"Aye, 'twas the birth."

Bridget opened her eyes again and met Francis's sympathetic gaze.

"But she loved you fiercely, little one. She said over and over that you were the best thing that had ever happened to her."

"What about my father?"

Francis looked away. "That I can't tell you."

"But if my mother was here, being cared for by the monks, she must have revealed who my father was."

"Your father was known to us."

"Then tell me who he was," she demanded, snatching her hand angrily from underneath his. "It's been twenty-two years, Brother. That's enough time for secrets to be honored."

"Some secrets must be kept forever. All I can tell you is that your father died shortly after your mother, and he left you to us as a sacred trust."

She could tell from the set of Francis's face that

once again she'd hit the wall of silence that had
greeted her inquiries ever since she could remember. It made little sense to her. And none of it explained why people had stared at her in the town,
unless her mother had been from there. "Do I look
like her?" she asked wistfully.

He smiled. "Aye, you're the image of her. She
was that beautiful."

Bridget was surprised. It was the first time that
any of the monks had ever made a comment on her
appearance. "Was she from Beauville? Is that why
people stared at me the other day?"

Francis shook his head. "This is the truth,
Bridget. I don't know who she was. But she was
not from Beauville."

"You didn't know her? Did no one here know
her identity?"

"Abbot Josef knew, but he swore never to reveal
it."

"Was she called Charlotte?"

The monk nodded. "Aye, that much I can tell
you."

It was not enough. For all these years she'd pre-
tended to herself that being a child of the abbey
was enough. The monks were her fathers and the
abbey was her heritage. But suddenly, her actual
parents had become real people. Her mother had a
name—Charlotte. She had lived and loved her baby

daughter for twelve whole days. And her father had left her to the monks as if she had been some kind of treasure to keep guarded and hidden.

Questions raced through her mind. Questions without answers. She had a sudden thought. "Did Abbot Josef reveal my mother's identity to someone before he died? Brother Alois, perhaps?"

Francis shifted on the narrow bench. "I've told you all I can, Bridget. Let that be an end to it. You're happy here at the abbey, and that's all that counts." He boosted himself up. "If we don't get these tables finished, we'll miss the sext prayers."

Bridget got slowly to her feet and started wiping down the row of tables once again, though her thoughts were not on cleaning. Brother Francis was right. She was happy at the abbey, but that was no longer all that counted. She wanted to know who she was.

Ranulf's head pounded as he unsaddled Thunder and led him into an empty stall in the abbey stables. He'd spent much of the afternoon talking with Jean the Smithy, but none of the smithy's information had given him any clues about what might have happened to his brother. Ranulf's only theory was that if Dragon had been seeking the black metal, then the man who might have the answer to his disappearance was Henri LeClerc. But Ranulf had learned his lesson blundering into the sheriff's house. He was not going to be so foolish as to ride up to Darmaux Castle alone.

"We need to get back to Lyonsbridge, boy," he told Thunder as he pulled the saddle blanket off his back.

"Are you planning to leave?" asked a soft voice from behind him.

He turned around to face Bridget. "I have to," he told her. "I need help."

"Have you found out something about your brother?"

"Maybe. I think his disappearance might have something to do with your monks' 'tinkerings,' as you call them."

Bridget looked puzzled. "You think he was coming here for their inventions?"

"For the black metal."

"I don't understand."

"I don't either, precisely. But what of your day? Did you speak with Francis?"

"Aye." She gave him a summary of her conversation with the monk.

"So the old woman who called you Charlotte must have known your mother?"

"Aye. Francis says it's foolhardy for me to go into town again, but I've been thinking all evening that I must risk it. I want to talk to the old dairy woman again.''

''And I was thinking that I should take you back to Lyonsbridge with me and leave you safely there while I come back with help to find Dragon.''

It was twilight outside and the interior of the stable was dim. Bridget could just barely see the sudden flare in his blue eyes. Her throat closed. His words had taken her completely by surprise. ''Take me to Lyonsbridge?'' she repeated.

''Aye. I don't like to leave you here unprotected. The sheriff's men may come looking for you, and no matter how much faith you place in them, I don't think your monks would put up a very good fight in your defense.''

She felt a pang of disappointment. She'd been foolish to think for even a moment that his offer had been anything more than a gallant gesture. Knights were sworn to protect helpless women. Any woman.

She drew herself up. ''What would your fine lady grandmother say if you suddenly appeared with a poor Norman girl with no name?''

Ranulf grinned. ''She'd say, *Bienvenue, ma chère*. She's Norman herself, remember?''

''A Norman *noblewoman*,'' Bridget pointed out. ''Nay, I thank you for the offer, but I'll stay right where I belong.''

"Which is an abbey full of old men?"

"Who have cared for me as fathers. Aye."

When she'd seen him riding in on Thunder, she'd followed him to the stables, wanting to tell him of her conversation with Francis. Now she was sorry she'd come. Her eyes misted with tears.

He saw them and before she could blink them away, he had put his arms around her. "Don't cry, angel," he murmured. "I'm sorry. I know how much the monks mean to you, but I find it difficult to stomach the idea of you living out your life here."

"It's the only home I know."

"Aye, but there's a whole world for you to *learn* to know."

"From the little I've seen of that world, I'm better off here."

His arms had brought her flat against the hardness of his body. "Were there no parts of that other world that you liked?" he asked, low in her ear.

"Aye, there were some parts," she answered, her voice even lower.

When she tipped her head to look up at him, he was smiling, and his eyes held another emotion that she had begun to know that afternoon in the woods. His lips brushed her cheek. "What would those parts be?" he asked.

"I think you know."

He shook his head and held her even more tightly so that her breasts flattened against his chest. "I want you to tell me," he murmured.

His lips nibbled at the tip of her chin. "This," she whispered.

His mouth moved to gnaw gently at her lower lip. "This?" he asked.

"Aye." The word came out as a sigh.

"Ah, angel, if you only knew," he breathed. "'Tis only the beginning."

Chapter Eleven

He took her mouth fully now, a deadly onslaught of lips and tongue, and she found it suddenly hard to stand upright. Sweeping her into his arms, he looked around the dark barn. "Hold on, sweetheart," he told her, then carried her through the row of stalls to the far corner where the fresh hay was piled. He set her on the ground with a quick, hard kiss on the lips and said, "Don't move."

Within moments, he'd hauled some saddle blankets from a rack on the wall and laid them out over the hay. When he was done, he looked back at the open stable door, which framed the last rays of the late spring twilight. "Will any of the monks be coming here this evening?" he asked her.

His voice reached her through a kind of fog. She shook her head. "They're at compline prayers. After that they go directly to bed."

"Good," he said. "Then we won't close the doors. I want to be able to see your eyes while I make love to you."

Her stomach did a flip at his words. "Are we going to make love?" she asked without the least tone of protest.

"Aye," he said, taking her in his arms again. "We are."

The idea was suddenly, deliciously enticing. She'd read about lovemaking in the forbidden abbey books, but she'd never thought it would happen to her. Somehow, with Ranulf's arms firmly around her, it felt natural and right and inevitable.

"I'd like that," she whispered.

He had little patience for their clothes, ridding first her, then himself, of any encumbrances. Finally they stood together naked, his hands moving slowly up and down the length of her back. Bridget closed her eyes and let her head fall back with a soft murmur of delight. "That feels exquisite," she said. "Like nothing I've ever known. Touching is mostly forbidden by the Rule here."

She'd had some quick embraces from the monks growing up, an occasional comforting hand on the shoulder. But in general, Ranulf's caresses were opening a whole new world of sensations. Her skin seemed to come alive everywhere he trailed his fingers.

"Everyone should be touched," he told her, moving his hands up to massage her shoulders and neck. "It's part of being human."

She opened her eyes and smiled at him in agreement. "Then I should touch you, as well."

"Aye," he agreed, his voice no longer steady.

For several minutes they explored each other, standing in the dimming light. He ran his hands up her arms and down her back to cup her small bottom, before lifting her closer against his stiffened manhood. The tips of her breasts brushed the crispy hairs of his chest and hardened.

She touched him tentatively at first, then more boldly, letting her hands sculpt the bulging line of his arms and slide along his sides to his narrow hips. He pulled back slightly and looked downward. "Touch me, angel," he said softly.

She moved her fingers to the center of him, softly stroking his hardness, and he did a swift intake of breath that made her exclaim, "Oh! I've not hurt you?"

With a low chuckle, he picked her up again and placed her on the blankets, then lay beside her. "Don't worry, you're doing everything just right, sweetheart," he said. "You've a naturally loving way about you."

Her skin felt flushed and peculiar waves were

radiating through her middle. "I don't know what to do exactly," she admitted.

"Do whatever feels good," he said. "Then relax and let me do what will make you feel good. It will all come about just as it should."

"Am I supposed to—"

He interrupted her words by laying his fingers across her lips, then swiped his hand across her forehead as if to clear her mind. "Stop thinking…." he murmured.

He started to kiss her again, and she discovered that he was right. Her thoughts were no longer coherent as his mouth wandered down to her nipples, and lingered there, sucking gently. His hand was making warm circles on her stomach, then lower as she lifted herself against his fingers.

By the time he moved over her, thought had fled entirely, replaced by a mindless wash of feeling. As he entered her, she was jolted by a slight sting, but the feeling was soon replaced by a delicious fullness that seemed to reach into her very core.

Their breathing had become uneven and agitated. Light flashed behind her closed eyelids, and an urgency began, a burning inside and out. She tightened her hold on Ranulf as he took her crashing over the top, then lay limp, dimly aware that he had withdrawn from her quickly to spill himself into the hay.

In an instant he was back, gathering her tenderly in his arms and rocking her slightly. "Angel," he whispered. "My beautiful angel of love."

She floated. Little by little the sensations subsided in her body and she came back to earth, aware of the feel of his skin sticking damply to hers, of the rough wool of the blanket against her back. It was long moments before she could speak.

"So that's what it's like to make love," she said dreamily.

Ranulf gave a shaky laugh. "That's what it's like if you've been touched by the gods. Normally, 'tis a bit less intense."

"Thank you," she whispered.

Ranulf shook his head, smiling. "You have to stop thanking me."

"But I'm grateful. I'm sorry that you had to go through your horrible bash on the head, but, just think. If you hadn't been wounded, you'd never have come here, and I'd never have known what this was like."

"I'd be bashed on the head any day if this was my reward. And I'm glad you liked it, too."

She burrowed her head into the crook of his neck. "I'll never forget it. Nor you, my very own knight."

The words had a sound of finality. A sudden chill went up her back as the evening breeze drifted in from the open doorway. He made no reply, merely tightening his hold on her. His breathing was evening out, and he appeared to be falling asleep. She lay silent for several moments, then said, "Ranulf?"

Sleepily he kissed the top of her head. "Aye, angel, I'm here. I apologize, but it appears that the long ride is catching up with me."

With a flush of guilt she pulled herself out of his arms. "Good Lord, I'd forgotten all about your wound. Are you sure you've done no damage?"

"My wound is fine, angel. 'Tis the rest of the body that appears to be fashed. The day has been long."

"And you should have long ago been back in your bed. What kept you in town?"

He told her of his long talk with the blacksmith, and by the time he was done, she'd moved away, sat up and started to put on her clothes.

"Is something the matter?" he asked, suddenly aware of her withdrawal.

"Do you think this man was telling you the truth?"

He looked puzzled. "Jean? Aye."

"So you believe him that the monks—*my* monks—make those terrible things? That they are working for this monster LeClerc, who killed the smithy's brother?"

Ranulf sat up slowly. The entire tone of her voice had changed. "Aye, Bridget. I believe that the weapons are being made here at the abbey. But I don't know who here is involved. It may be all the monks or it may be just a few."

Bridget had finished dressing. She turned to face him. "Well, I don't believe it."

"There's no other furnace powerful enough to forge such a metal. I've never seen anything like it in all Europe or England."

"Then someone else is using it. I can't believe the monks know anything about it."

He shook his head. "Be reasonable, angel. The monks swarm over this work shed all day long. How could someone else be using the blast fire without their knowledge?"

Her chin went up in that stubborn way he recognized. "I don't know, but 'tis not possible that the brothers of St. Gabriel are warmongers and murderers. I'll never warrant such a tale."

Ranulf sighed, then explained with a touch of exasperation, "But 'tis not *your* brother who is missing, Bridget. I must investigate every possibility to find Dragon."

Her expression softened. "Aye, I know. And you may find answers with the sheriff and the Baron of Darmaux. I just don't think you'll find them here at the abbey."

He finished fastening his belt around his waist, then reached to take her hand. "Will you come with me to wait at Lyonsbridge while I return with help to solve this mystery?"

She shook her head slowly. "My place is here with the monks."

He looked at the tousled blankets on top of the hay mound. "Even when you have seen some of the wonder that the rest of the world has to offer?" he asked softly.

"Aye," she said. "What I see of the world is that it holds out enticements to cloud your thinking while it tries to bring hurt to the people you love."

He hadn't believed that she would really refuse to leave with him, especially now. The thought of having to leave her unprotected made his tone sharper than he had intended. "I don't want to hurt anyone, Bridget. I just want to find my brother."

"Your brother is a knight, like you, Ranulf. This is a place of peace. You'll not find him here."

The sky outside had grown black, and he could barely see her face, but he heard the anger in her voice. He tried to think of something to say to bring back some of the feelings they'd shared only moments before as they'd lain together on the hay, but before he could speak, she whirled around and ran out of the barn.

* * *

"He is well again?" the baron asked the cowled figure who had met him in the woods behind St. Gabriel.

"Aye. He leaves in the morning to ride to his home at Lyonsbridge, but he says he only returns home to bring more help to add to the search," the monk said.

"And the girl is hidden with you again."

"Aye, she's returned home."

LeClerc snapped his whip against his leg. "She's become a danger to us."

"She knows nothing, and she wants nothing more than to live here in peace as she always has. It was part of our bargain."

"Aye, but the bargain may have to change. We can't afford to have people snooping around the abbey until the entire shipment for the duke is finished."

"I know, milord, but I tell you the girl won't be a problem."

"We'll see. In the meantime, we'll get rid of the Englishman."

"You won't try to do it inside the abbey?" the monk asked.

"Nay, 'tis unnecessary and unwise. Such a crime could lead to an investigation from the bishopric— meddling that we've so far managed to avoid."

"I agree. 'Tis best if the knight is well away

from the abbey before you strike. We'll have to hope that this time your men prove more effective than the first time.''

LeClerc walked over to his horse and pulled himself impatiently into the saddle. "Guise is a bumbling fool. This time I intend to be sure that the job is done right myself."

The monk gave a slight bow. "Very good, milord. As long as he has left the abbey well behind before you deal with him."

"Let me worry about the Englishman, Brother. It's your job to keep things peaceful here and keep the monks away from the shed at night while my men are at work. The duke is expecting his weapons soon."

The monk nodded.

LeClerc pulled up on the reins of his horse and the animal reared back. "And remember, if the girl starts causing trouble, we'll be forced to get rid of her, too."

"I understand, milord," the monk said.

The baron wheeled his horse around and rode off into the trees.

Bridget had been awake since long before dawn, lying in her bed, her mind tumbling. She tried to keep from remembering the feeling of Ranulf's hands on her in the stable the previous evening, but the treacherous thoughts kept surfacing, along with an irrational desire for a repetition of the experience. Then she'd remember how the evening had ended, how he'd accused the monks of complicity in weapon making and murder.

Before the roosters started crowing in the pen behind the stable, she rose and made her way to the kitchen. She hoped Francis would join her to help with morning chores. It was often his custom, though Bridget suspected his presence was due more to a desire for an early breakfast than to his devotion to work.

She was relieved to see his round form turning toward her as she went into the kitchen. "Brother Francis, I'm so glad you're here," she said.

The monk licked a last bit of butter from his fingers and asked, "What is it, child?"

"It's...oh...*everything,*" she ended, biting her lip to keep back the tears.

Francis immediately put down the bread he'd been eating and walked over to her. "Sit down, Bridget. Tell me what has happened."

Her cheeks flamed as she realized that she could never tell Francis the most momentous thing that had happened to her in the past twenty-four hours, but she did tell him about Ranulf's charges regarding the blast fire.

As she finished her account, Francis sat heavily on the bench beside her, his face grim.

"What is it, Brother Francis?" she asked. "Surely you can't think that there is any truth to these accusations. Weapons at St. Gabriel? Why, the very idea is ridiculous."

Francis remained silent for such a long time that Bridget finally said again, "'Tis a ridiculous notion, is it not?"

"I'm not sure."

Bridget felt a pulsing behind her ears. "What do you mean?" she asked slowly.

Francis looked over at her. "I've never been comfortable about the blast fire since they built the confounded thing. And I do think a great deal of metal is produced there. I don't know what happens to it. It seems to...disappear."

Their gazes held. "But how could—" she began.

"I don't know," Francis said.

"Someone must know," she said.

"Aye, someone must know."

"We need to call a meeting and ask."

Francis shook his head. "If one of the brothers of St. Gabriel is keeping this secret and has allied himself with the Baron of Darmaux, 'tis not likely that he will admit it before all."

"Ranulf intends to bring reinforcements from England and go against the baron with force."

Francis shook his head and sighed. "If someone here is involved, it could mean the end of St. Gabriel."

Bridget felt cold inside. "We must discover who it is and somehow stop him. If no one in the abbey will cooperate, the baron will have to look elsewhere for his weapons."

Francis nodded. "I'm going out to the work shed right now. Perhaps I can find out something before anyone else is awake. But what about Ranulf?"

Bridget's face became determined. "I believe I can convince our English knight to delay his homecoming while you see what you can discover."

Francis nodded and heaved himself up from the bench. "This, um, *delaying tactic* would not involve anything that would later require the confessional, would it, child?" he asked gently.

Bridget's cheeks flamed once again at the monk's perceptive question. Was it obvious that she and Ranulf had already made love? "Nay, Brother Francis, I promise you. I'm merely going to ask his assistance on a certain matter."

Francis stood watching her a minute more, then appeared to be satisfied. "Good," he said. "Ranulf seems to be a fine person, but he's a nobleman, and they are not always known for their scruples in dealing with…er…lower classes."

His words hit her like a blow in the midsection,

but she managed a smile. "Don't worry," she said. "I know better than to think that Ranulf Brand could ever be meant for the likes of me."

"I'd go by myself if you hadn't been so insistent that I was in danger from the sheriff's men," Bridget told Ranulf as she sat next to him on his cot. The monks had already all awakened and left the dormitory, and they were alone.

"I don't think the old dairy woman even knows her own name, much less your mother's," Ranulf said. He was embarrassed at being caught still abed at this late morning hour, and he was uncertain about Bridget's sudden change of attitude. When she'd left him the previous evening, she'd been angry. Now she seemed all sweetness, though she had resisted his attempt to reach for her hand and draw her near him on the bed.

"I have to at least try," she said. "She called me Charlotte, which we know now was my mother's first name. At some time in the past, Mistress Courmier must have known my mother's family name, as well."

Ranulf pushed himself around her on the bed and reached for his tunic to pull on over his underclothes. "I wanted you to come with me today to Lyonsbridge," he argued.

"And by the time I returned from England, old Mistress Courmier may be dead, which would mean that I'd lost my last chance to find out what she knew about me."

"Her son, Pierre, said he had no idea why she called you Charlotte. He seemed to know nothing about the name."

"Pierre is only a few years older than I. He probably wouldn't remember if the family somehow knew my mother."

Ranulf finished dressing quickly, trying to decide what he should do. Now that he'd seen the black metal and learned of the involvement of the sheriff and Baron LeClerc, he was anxious to get home, tell his news to his grandparents and recruit his brother Thomas's help. On the other hand, he was relieved that Bridget seemed to have gotten over her anger, and riding with her today to question the Courmiers might give him the opportunity to convince her to return to England with him.

"Very well," he said. "Let's start immediately before we lose more of the day."

"I'm not the one who lay as a slugabed the entire morning," she pointed out with an impish smile.

He wanted desperately to kiss her, but things were not the same between them as they had been in the darkened barn, so instead he touched a light finger to her nose and said, "'Tis not fair to make fun of a knight recovering from battle."

He gave a wry twist to the remark, leaving open to interpretation exactly which battle he meant.

Chapter Twelve

Pierre Courmier greeted Bridget and Ranulf cordially enough as they rode up to his dairy farm. Ranulf felt his courtesy was commendable since the last time they'd appeared it had been to involve him in the aftermath of the Marchands' tragedy.

"Mistress Marchand is safely on her way to Rouen," he told them as Ranulf dismounted from Thunder and reached up to assist Bridget. "Her daughter came for her yesterday. She's left the selling of the cottage in my hands."

Ranulf reached to warmly clasp the dairyman's hand. "One can see that you're a man to rely on, Pierre. I'm beholden to you."

"No need. 'Twas the thing to do among neighbors."

"Nevertheless, we're grateful for your help," Bridget added.

Pierre gave her a bright smile. "I was pleased to be of service. The Marchands were fine folk."

Bridget's smile faded. "Aye, they were."

"But we've come on another matter," Ranulf said quickly, watching his companion's face. "Do you remember in the market the other day when your mother called this lady by name?"

"Aye, 'twas Charlotte, I recollect. But as I told you, my mother's not too clear in the head these days."

"Would it upset her if we asked her some questions?" Ranulf tied Thunder to a fence that surrounded the dairyman's neat vegetable garden.

"I never know. Sometimes she becomes kind of jumpy when she's trying to remember something." He looked over at Bridget, whose eyes were pleading, then said, "I suppose you can try."

"If she gets upset, we'll stop," Bridget told him.

He nodded in agreement and led them into the big stone farmhouse. "Mind the door," he told Ranulf, pointing to the knight's tall head, though he was nearly as tall himself. Both men had to stoop to fit under the low lintel.

The inside of the house was brightly lit with windows cut on three sides. A door led from the large main room to additional rooms at the back of the house. The Courmiers were obviously a prosperous family, Ranulf observed.

There was no one in the room they entered. "My brothers are out in the barns," Pierre explained. "And my mother is lying down for a nap."

"Then we should not disturb her," Bridget said, concerned.

"Nay, 'tis time for her to be up and about for a while. I'll go fetch her." He motioned to a bench. "Please have a seat."

Ranulf looked around for signs of children's playthings, but found nothing. It appeared that the Courmier brothers were bachelors. "How many sisters and brothers do you have?" he asked.

Pierre grinned. "No sister would have ever survived this household. We're six lads."

"Six!" Bridget exclaimed. Ranulf gave her a sympathetic glance. It must be hard to picture a house full of siblings after the lonely childhood she had spent. He couldn't imagine what his life would have been like without his two brothers for company.

"Aye, six. The brawling and brawny Courmiers, they call us."

"You outman my household two to one," Ranulf said. "But my two brothers and I would make you worthy opponents in a round of wrestling."

The two men exchanged a typically male look of competition. "Maybe we can arrange a match sometime." Pierre grinned, then added, "I'll be right back with my mother."

"Thomas and Dragon and I could probably take on the whole crew at once," Ranulf said with a flare of bravado when the dairyman disappeared into the back.

Bridget laughed. "You sound like the monks when they're trying to best each other with their tinkerings. But at least they don't end up with broken crowns for their pains." She pointed to his still-bandaged head.

He gave a rueful smile. "Aye, we men are barbarians, aren't we? Though 'twas not exactly a friendly competition that got me this wound."

"I know."

They turned as Pierre reappeared in the door, his arm around an old woman scarcely half his height. Mistress Courmier looked even more frail and vague than when they had seen her in the market, and Bridget's heart fell. It didn't appear likely that the old dairy woman would be able to help her.

Pierre helped his mother get settled in a chair that was obviously designed just for her comfort. It was short enough for her tiny legs to reach the floor and had sturdy slats up the side to keep her from falling. When she was seated, she leaned toward the visitors. "Have they given you a raisin cake?" she croaked.

Bridget was too startled to answer, but Ranulf said politely, "We've no need of refreshment, good mother. We just came to talk with you."

"I try and try to teach these boys their manners, but they forget about the raisin cakes," she said with a sigh.

"We've eaten already," Ranulf told the woman in a slightly louder voice. Bridget's hopes were sinking lower.

Pierre knelt next to his mother's chair and laid a reassuring hand on her arm. "Sir Ranulf and Mistress Bridget have come to see you, Mother," he said.

"Of course they have. She comes every Sabbath Day," Camille said, pointing to Bridget. She turned to her son. "And we give them raisin cakes."

Pierre lifted his head sharply. "I remember that," he said with a look of wonder.

Ranulf reached for Bridget's hand and gave it a squeeze. She remained frozen on the bench. "What exactly do you remember, my friend?" Ranulf asked.

Pierre shook his head as if to clear it. "I was just a little boy, perhaps only five or six. But I remember the fancy lady who used to come to see my mother. I remember that I always liked the way she smelled."

"And you think that woman was the Charlotte

your mother was talking about in the market?''
Ranulf asked.

"My Charlotte," said the old woman. "My little
lamb who I raised from a child."

The others in the room exchanged a confused
glance. "You say you had no sisters," Ranulf confirmed, looking at Pierre.

The dairyman was staring into space. "I'm trying to remember the woman who came to visit. I
believe that before she married my father, my
mother had spent several years as this woman's
nurse."

"Then this lady was a woman of some means,"
Ranulf confirmed with another squeeze of Bridget's
hand.

Bridget had grown cold and trembly inside. Suddenly she wondered if she really wanted to know
the truth about her birth. Would she remain the
same person? Would knowing the name of her parents make her life any better? Or might the knowledge bring changes that she could not predict?

Pierre was still lost in memory. "The lady Charlotte," he said slowly. "Aye, my father used to
speak of the lady Charlotte."

"My precious child," Camille said. "They
killed her. They killed my lovely Charlotte. I tried
to warn her...." A single tear made its way out of

the corner of her eye and zigzagged along the wrinkles of her face.

Ranulf looked at Pierre, who shrugged. "I'm sorry," he said. "I don't remember anything about that. I just know that the visits stopped one day. I hadn't thought of them in years."

"Would any of your brothers remember more?" Ranulf asked.

"I don't think so. I'm the oldest."

Bridget felt almost as if she were in a trance. She rose from the bench and walked across the room to kneel in front of the old woman's chair. Pierre stood and moved back to make room for her. Taking the woman's hands in her own, she said gently, "No one killed Charlotte, dear one. She died giving me birth."

"I couldn't save her," the old woman wailed, rocking. "If I had kept her from *them,* I could have saved her."

"Nay, 'twas the childbirth killed her. But she lives on through me. I'm Charlotte's daughter."

The woman's faded blue eyes suddenly took on a bright gleam of lucidity. "In truth?" she asked. "You are my Charlotte's child?"

"Aye," Bridget said, and when the old woman leaned forward, she lifted herself up to embrace her. "Put no fault on yourself for her death, for 'twas the Lord decided to take her life in exchange for mine.''

Camille cupped Bridget's face in her hands. "Aye, ye are the very likeness of her, child. Just as beautiful.''

Bridget took a shaky breath, then asked, "Do you remember her family name? The place where you cared for her?''

Camille looked surprised. "Why, I cared for her at her home, of course. At Darmaux. My baby was Charlotte LeClerc, and I cared for her at Darmaux Castle.''

The dairyman gave a low whistle. "I don't know the connection, but Charlotte can't have been the current Baron of Darmaux's daughter. He's not old enough.''

"Could she have been his sister?'' Ranulf asked.

Bridget felt sick. Somehow, this is what she had been dreading since the old woman had first entered the room. What if she found out who she really was and found it unbearable? Could she really be connected to this wicked person who traded in weapons and had been responsible for the death of poor old Mr. Marchand and Jean the Smithy's brother? Could this horrible man be her *uncle?* She sent Ranulf a stricken glance, and saw that he was reading her thoughts.

"We know nothing yet for sure,'' he said firmly.

Raising his voice, he asked Camille, "Who was Charlotte, good mother? What connection did she have to Darmaux?"

But the old woman's mind had receded once again into her memories. She patted Bridget's cheek gently. "My beautiful Charlotte," she said. "You must eat more. For the babe." She turned to her son. "Bring the lady Charlotte a raisin cake, Pierre."

"Aye, Mama," he said.

She gave a satisfied nod, then closed her eyes and seemed to drift off. After a moment, Pierre said, "I'm afraid she may be tired. She rarely sees visitors these days."

Bridget stood, then leaned over to place a soft kiss on Camille's cheek. "Thank you for loving my mother," she whispered. When she straightened up, her eyes were bright with unshed tears.

The sight gave Ranulf a twinge. Once again he tried to imagine a childhood without his family, without Lyonsbridge. He stood and walked swiftly across the room to put his arm around Bridget.

Pierre moved to his mother's side and straightened her in the chair. "I wish I could remember more," he said with a sympathetic glance at Bridget.

"You've been a great help," Ranulf told him. "We're grateful."

Pierre escorted them outside and stood watching while they mounted Thunder and rode away. For several moments, neither spoke.

Finally Ranulf said over his shoulder, "'Tis a start. Now that you know something, you may be able to find out more and perhaps learn about your father."

She tightened her hold on his waist. "If my family is responsible for Philip Marchand's death, I don't think I want to know more about them."

Ranulf had no answer. From what he knew of the Baron of Darmaux, he would want no part of the family, either.

"The monk says that there've been questions about the black metal." Sheriff Guise had ridden to Darmaux Castle before dawn and had been shown into the baron's bedchamber.

LeClerc swung his legs out of bed. "Who's asking questions?"

"One of the other brothers, apparently. But I suspect the Englishman's behind it. I think it's time we go in there and get rid of him."

The baron uttered an oath. "I've told the duke that we'd have the next shipment of weapons to him in a fortnight. We can't afford to interrupt the production now."

"It's going to be interrupted anyway if they discover our nighttime activities at the furnace."

LeClerc appeared lost in thought. "The Englishman still hasn't left St. Gabriel?"

"Nay. I have a watch on the road to the coast."

"He needs to be disposed of, but I'd still prefer not to do it at the abbey. Set some guards around the complex. The minute he sets foot outside the walls, seize him."

"What about the monks asking questions?"

"Let them ask, the doddering old fools. Even if they do discover that one of their holy brotherhood has been helping us manufacture weapons, they're not likely to do anything about it. They're a bunch of old men in skirts who can think of nothing more than their prayers and their tinkering. And our man will keep things calm."

The sheriff looked less convinced. "What if some of them take it upon themselves to go to the bishopric with the information?"

"Nay, they're a complacent bunch. They've lived peacefully without interference from the church all these years. They won't risk changing that." LeClerc had finished pulling on his overtunic and surcoat. "Is the Englishman's brother dead?"

"I've sent a man to Mordin Castle to order it done," the sheriff answered.

LeClerc nodded. "Too bad, once the secret of

the black metal is known, he would have brought a good ransom. Lyonsbridge is a wealthy estate.''

"Well, 'tis done now. The messenger should be on his way there with the order.''

"Good. I trust both the Brand brothers will be eliminated quickly." He picked up his leather belt from a rack and twisted it in his hands like a garrote. "Then we'll see to the matter of my late cousin's daughter.''

Bridget sought out Francis as soon as they got back to the abbey. The monk was just returning from the path to the work shed.

"What have you been able to discover?" she asked.

His face was grave. "I spent most of the afternoon around the blast fire," he told her. "Nearly drove Cyril and Ebert crazy. I simply can't believe that either one of them could be involved in something like this, but now that I was looking for it, I did see plenty of evidence that someone has been producing substantial amounts of the metal.''

"Then it's possible that it may be true.''

"More than possible. I also found this." He'd been holding his hands folded together in the sleeves of his habit. He pulled one out to show her that he held a piece of black metal narrowed to a point.

"What's that?" she asked as a feeling of cold swept through her.

"Part of a weapon, I should think, a point of some kind." He turned it over in his hands. "I'd judge it too long for an arrow, so it must be for a lance. 'Tis sharp as a dagger and from what I could see when I tested it against a rock, harder than any metal known."

"Hard enough to pierce armor, as Ranulf said?"

"I'm a man of peace, not of war, but I think 'tis possible."

Bridget felt sick. She took the shiny black spear point from him and looked down at it as if it were a serpent. "You say you found it?"

"Aye, fallen on the floor behind some of the other equipment."

"Did you ask Cyril and Ebert about it?"

"Not yet. I thought perhaps I should talk to Alois first, and I think I'll pay a nighttime call to the work shed. If someone from outside of St. Gabriel is using the work shed to make weapons, it must be while none of us are there."

The monks spent the evening and early morning hours in prayers and slept during the night, which left a large amount of time that the work shed was supposed to be standing empty.

"Will you go tonight?" she asked.

"Aye, and in the morning I'll talk to the abbot."

Bridget had a terrible moment of doubt. Even before he had become abbot, Alois had always seemed different from the others, more detached. "You don't think that Brother Alois could be part of this, do you?"

Francis did not share her misgivings. He shook his head firmly. "Alois has been our leader for years. Why would he betray the brotherhood in that way?"

The idea seemed unthinkable to Bridget, as well, but it was equally unthinkable that any of the other monks would be involved. Ebert was the monk who had the most contact with the outside world, but he was friendly and easygoing. She couldn't imagine him as a participant in trading weapons. Cyril was so involved in his science that he often forgot to eat the noon meal. In fact, the only interruption of his work he would tolerate was Bridget herself. For her, he always had a smile and a kind word. Cyril loved her, just as all the monks did. She couldn't bear to think of any of them as a traitor.

"We must find out the truth of this matter," she said with a note of desperation. "Ranulf wants to be off to Lyonsbridge and will return with a veritable army of Englishmen. Then what will become of us?"

Francis shook his head. "I'd like for us to be

able to solve this mystery ourselves. Do you think you could persuade him to delay a little longer?''

The cursed blush flamed her cheeks as she thought about the most surefire way to keep Ranulf from leaving the abbey, which would be a repetition of the lovemaking they'd shared the night in the barn. Of course, she would never seriously entertain such a notion. Anyway, she told herself, now that Ranulf had made love to her once, perhaps he would no longer be interested.

''I'll delay him,'' she said with a lift of her chin. ''One way or another.''

Francis appeared too distracted about the distressing events to notice her self-consciousness. ''Good,'' he said. ''By tomorrow we may know something more.''

Changing the subject, she briefly told Francis about their discovery regarding her apparent connection to the Baron of Darmaux. He appeared unsurprised, but swore that he knew nothing more about the lady Charlotte's identity.

''I did know that she was a noblewoman,'' he admitted. ''Brother Josef told us all that due to unusual circumstances, the abbey would provide shelter to her while she gave birth to her child. He never revealed what those circumstances were.''

''But you knew the identity of the father,''

Bridget protested. "If you would tell me that, it might give some clue."

Francis hesitated, then finally said, "I can assure you, lass, that your father had no connection to Darmaux Castle, nor would it tell you anything more if I revealed his name."

She tried arguing further, but he wouldn't budge from his position. Finally she gave up and asked, "Would you like me to go with you to the work shed tonight?"

"Nay. You deal with Ranulf. I'm going only to observe. I'll not get myself into any trouble."

They agreed to meet in the kitchen before dawn to decide on their next move. Then she wished him good luck and started walking slowly back to her little house. She still held the spear point, and her fingers rubbed over and over its smoothness. If someone at the abbey was making weapons, it had to be stopped, and that might mean that it would be impossible to preserve the life she had always known here.

But if there was a way to protect it, she would. And she would start by keeping Ranulf from leaving for Lyonsbridge.

Chapter Thirteen

A yellow, nearly full moon was rising in the midnight sky when Francis made his way out to the work shed. Compline prayers were long finished and the monks had retired. Francis had lain for nearly an hour, feigning sleep, then had risen and gone all through the dormitory, checking the neat rows of beds. Every one appeared to be occupied.

He felt a little foolish creeping about in the middle of the night, but as he neared the work shed, he could hear the roar of the blast fire and it strengthened his resolve. If there was treachery at St. Gabriel, he was going to find out about it.

The double doors to the shed stood wide-open. Inside, light flared again and then again as the big furnace was fired. Someone was inside.

Noiselessly, in his monk's sandals, he crept to the north side of the door and peered around the edge. On the far side of the shed he could see figures moving about in the eerie light of the furnace. There were at least six men and, to Francis's immense relief, none were dressed in the habit of a monk.

He flattened himself against the wall as he suddenly heard the sound of voices coming from the path to the abbey behind him. Sliding sideways so that he was hidden behind the big shed door, he waited for the newcomers' approach.

"The baron wants this finished quickly," one of the voices said.

Francis peered through the crack in the door. The men's faces were illuminated by the furnace light coming from inside. He recognized the speaker as the sheriff from Beauville and, with a sinking heart, he recognized the man the sheriff was addressing. It was Brother Cyril.

"The men can only produce so many points a night," Cyril was saying in that animated, special voice he used for discussing his scientific achievements. "If you cheat on the time or the mixture, you won't be happy with the results."

The sheriff grumbled his reply. "I don't know why we can't just come in here and take over the furnace. Then we could be producing night and day."

"You promised you wouldn't violate the sanctity of the abbey," Cyril protested.

"Aye, because the Duke of Austria wanted to keep his new weapons secret. But once he starts using them in his next campaign, everyone in the world will know of the marvelous black metal of St. Gabriel."

Francis thought that Cyril looked distressed, but it could have been the way the furnace flares fell on his face.

"What will happen then?" the monk asked.

The sheriff clapped a heavy hand on the monk's shoulder. "Why, then you'll be famous, Brother. 'Tis what you wanted, isn't it? For the world to know how brilliant you are?"

"Aye, I wanted the world to have my knowledge," Cyril said. "But I didn't think it would mean the end of the abbey."

"Ah, well, it's a bit late to worry about it now, isn't it?"

The men reached the edge of the door where Francis was hiding. Absently the sheriff reached out with his hand to push it open a little farther, but with Francis wedged behind, it sprang back at him.

"What the hell?" the sheriff exclaimed. Francis made a sound as the door hit flat against his big belly. Then, before he could even think to run, the sheriff had pulled the door open and pinned him against the wall.

"Brother Francis!" Cyril cried.

"Who's this?" the sheriff growled. He pushed against Francis's throat with his metal wristlet, nearly choking him.

"'Tis one of the brothers," Cyril said.

"What's he doing here?"

"I don't know. I've told no one about this." Cyril's voice was shaky. "Don't hurt him," he added.

Guise eased the pressure against Francis's neck. "What are you doing here, lard bucket?" he asked.

Francis coughed, then said to Cyril, "I've come to learn who has betrayed our abbey, Brother Cyril, and I warrant that now I know."

The sheriff muttered an oath and turned his head toward Cyril. "How many more know your secret, Brother?"

Cyril shook his head in misery.

"Everyone will know of it if I have anything to say about it," Francis said.

The sheriff gave a disgusted look from Francis to Cyril. "Confounded godmongers," he said. Then, still holding Francis pinned against the wall with his big arm, he drew a dagger from his belt and moved it toward Francis's throat.

Cyril was on him in an instant, pulling the hand

with the dagger away from Francis's neck. "No!" he shouted.

Guise released himself from the monk's grasp without effort. Then he pulled his arm back and thrust the knife into Francis's habit.

Cyril watched in horror as the round monk sank to the ground without a sound.

Guise pulled back his dagger, wiped it on his tunic and stepped around the still-open door. "You have until dawn to bury your fat friend," he told Cyril, "unless you want all your precious abbey brothers to discover that you helped cause the death of one of their number."

Cyril had clutched the side of the door for support. "You've killed him," he gasped.

"Aye, and he's only the first this night. With luck, we'll have taken care of the two bloody Englishmen as well before the night's out."

"May you burn in hell, Guise," the monk said, crossing himself.

The sheriff laughed. "Aye, but you'll join me there. After all, Brother, who is the greater murderer, the one who dispatches one bothersome monk with a single dagger or the one who invents a metal that will cause the deaths of hundreds, perhaps thousands?" Then he turned and stalked into the work shed.

* * *

The half-open door blocked the light from reaching where Francis had fallen. Cyril knelt beside him and felt his body in the darkness. The entire right side of the monk's habit was wet with blood, but when he touched him, Francis gave a slight groan.

"Francis!" Cyril said in an excited whisper. "Can you hear me?"

"Aye." He opened his eyes. "'Tis as I've always said, sometimes a bit of bulk can serve a man in good stead. The knave's knife just nicked my side."

"You're bleeding."

"'Tis only a scratch."

"Francis, I never thought it would come to this. I never wanted to put the abbey in danger."

"Nay, but what about all the soldiers you were condemning to death with your devil's tools?"

Cyril had no reply.

"'Tis not the time to speak of it," Francis said after a moment. "I need to get this side bandaged or I truly shall bleed to death. Will you help me?"

"Aye," Cyril said, his tone heavy with remorse.

"And then we need to find Ranulf. What did the sheriff mean when he said that two Englishmen would die? Was he talking about Ranulf?"

"Aye, and his brother. They've had him captive for months since he came seeking information about the black metal."

"Ah, Cyril, how could you have put yourself in league with such men?"

"It started because I just wanted…" Cyril's voice faded until Francis could barely hear him. "I just wanted my discovery to be known to the world. The baron offered to help me in exchange for my silence."

"We don't have time to discuss it now. Help me up, and then let's get away from here before the sheriff discovers that it takes more than his puny dagger to kill this lard bucket."

The knock on her door was soft, but Bridget had no trouble hearing it, nor recognizing the low voice that called to her from outside. "Are you still awake?" Ranulf asked.

She'd thought that he'd already gone to sleep, which had relieved her, since it would mean she wouldn't have to worry about her delaying tactics until the following day. Crossing to open the door, she answered, "Aye, I'm awake."

He was fully dressed and didn't look the least bit tired in spite of their long ride and the late hour. "I came to try to persuade you one last time to ride to Lyonsbridge with me," he said.

She shook her head. "Nay, the monks need me here. Nor should you be going. Your wound's not healed enough for the crossing."

Ranulf smiled. "My wound is fine, thanks to my angel nurse. I don't like to leave you, sweetheart. We don't know when the sheriff's men will begin to search for you again."

"They won't come here," she said, opening the door more widely and gesturing for him to come in. "When are you planning to leave?"

"Now," he said, stepping into the room.

"Tonight?" she asked in alarm. Then, aware that her tone sounded panicky, she said more calmly, "You can't ride in the dark."

"There's a full moon. Thunder and I will be fine, and we can be at the coast before dawn. With luck, I'll be back here in two days, three at most, with a full contingent of Lyonsbridge men. Then we can really see what LeClerc is up to."

Bridget's heart had begun to race. "But why the hurry? Surely it would be better to wait and go in the daylight?"

"Nay, I've delayed too long already." He reached out and took both her hands. "Sweetheart, somehow I know that Dragon is out there somewhere waiting for me to find him. He's waited long enough."

"But—" She searched her mind to think of arguments to sway him, all the while aware of his warm hands clasping her cold ones. Finally she decided to voice her fears directly. "What will become of the abbey if you bring all those men back here? What will happen to the monks?''

Ranulf looked uncomfortable, but answered, ''Bridget, if your monks are involved in making weapons to kill people, they don't deserve to be able to continue on under the name of a holy order.''

''So you would see an end to St. Gabriel?''

''If necessary.''

She pulled her hands away. ''I'd like you to give me and Francis some time to find the truth of this matter.''

Ranulf looked surprised. ''Does Francis think he may know something of it?''

She shook her head. ''Nay, but he's going to put the question to the abbot tomorrow and perhaps talk to some of the others. If you'll give us some time, we may be able to come up with some answers for you.''

''Meanwhile, Dragon waits.''

Bridget swallowed hard. ''If he's waited this long, what difference would a few more days make?''

Ranulf's expression was sad. ''I don't know what difference it might make. That's why I have to go get help now. Do you think I like leaving you unprotected? But I need help. I'm just one man.

There's no way I can go up against the sheriff and LeClerc all by myself.''

Bridget looked straight into his blue eyes. "I'm asking you to wait," she said.

He hesitated a long moment, but finally said, "Angel, I can't."

Inside she felt shaky. Backing up to the candle stand by her cot, she reached behind her to retrieve the spear point she'd left there earlier. "Do I get a kiss goodbye?" she asked.

Ranulf cocked his head in surprise, then smiled and said, "I make it a practice never to deny a kiss to an angel."

In two steps he had her in his arms and the next thing she knew, his lips were on hers. She steeled herself not to be affected, but her knees went weak as his soft tongue swiped along her bottom lip. In another instant, she would be incapable of action.

Gripping the spear point firmly in her hand, she brought it up so that the point was pressed into his neck. "Don't move," she said firmly, "because this is very sharp."

She felt his body go tense. "What game is this?" he asked.

"'Tis no game," she said. "I made a simple request and you refused. Now 'tis no longer a request, but an order. I want you to sit down on the bed behind you—carefully now or I'm apt to prick you.''

Rather to her amazement, he complied with her request without protest. She kept the spear point pressed against him as he moved, then backed carefully away, holding it in ready. He watched her with a dark expression. ''Has this all been a charade?'' he asked. ''Are you part of this conspiracy?''

She was surprised at the question. ''I'm part of no conspiracy, Ranulf. I'm merely trying to protect my monks from being overrun by two armies— yours and the baron's.''

Her answer seemed to relieve him. He pushed himself back on the bed, the ghost of a smile playing about his lips. ''So you intend to keep me prisoner here?'' he asked.

She nodded. ''For a while. Until Francis has determined what goes on in the work shed at night.''

''And you think that scrap is enough to hold me here?'' he asked, pointing to the metal in her hand.

She looked down at it. '''Tis wickedly sharp. It could tear you open like a wildcat's claw.''

''Well now, we wouldn't want that to happen, would we?''

Bridget bit her lip. She felt a little foolish standing in front of him with her piece of weapon clutched in her fingers, and she couldn't stand here all night guarding him. Ranulf seemed to have relaxed. He sat leaning with his back against the wall, his long legs stretched out the length of the bed. He continued to watch her with a little twist of a smile.

"Will you give me your word that you won't leave if I let you go?" she asked finally.

He gave a slow, almost imperceptible, shake of his head. "Nay," he said.

She swallowed again. Her entire throat had gone dry. *By St. Bridget, I should have waited for Francis,* she told herself. "Lie down, then," she ordered. His eyebrows lifted in surprise. She made a horizontal gesture with the spear point. "Lie down on the cot," she repeated. "I'm not letting you go anywhere, so you might as well be comfortable for the night."

His big body dwarfed her small bed, but he stretched and lay back against the mattress. "Like this?" he asked.

There was a gleam in his eyes as he looked up at her that was making her stomach do those peculiar flips she had come to know. She avoided looking at him as she opened her chest of belongings and took out some hair ribbons that Brother Ebert had bought for her at the market in a rare acknowledgment of her needs as a young woman. The gesture had meant the world to her.

She looked doubtfully down at the silky strands in her hand. They seemed flimsy compared to the ropes the monks used to tie up animals in the stable, but she had nothing else in her room that would serve.

She could see the easy rise and fall of Ranulf's broad chest. He didn't look the least bit distressed, whereas her own breathing had become quick and shallow and there was a pounding behind her ears.

''Er…if you won't give me your word not to try to leave, I'll have to bind you to keep you here,'' she told him. He continued to watch her, eyes dancing in the candlelight. With a grimace of distaste, she put the spear point temporarily between her teeth to free her hands, then stepped closer to the bed.

At a gesture from her, he cooperated by putting both his hands above his head. His gaze never left her face.

Kneeling, she lifted his limp arm, tied a loop around his wrist and fastened the other end of the ribbon to the leg of the cot. Then she walked around the back end of the bed to tie the other hand to the opposite side. Once it was done, she straightened up and took the spear point out of her mouth with a sigh of relief. ''There,'' she said. ''Will you be able to sleep all right like that?'' she asked, moving around the bed to look at him again.

"You do love this place, don't you?" he asked softly.

She'd been so concerned with her attempts to restrain him that she hardly understood his question, but after a moment she realized that he was referring to St. Gabriel. "Aye," she told him. "Every bit as much as you love your Lyonsbridge."

He winced. "Bridget, I don't want to bring hurt to you or any of the ones you love, but something is wrong here. I believe something evil has entered your peaceful world, and nothing will be the same until you root out what it is and set it right."

"That's what Francis and I are trying to do."

He shook his head. "There's no way you and Francis can prove a match for someone as powerful as LeClerc."

"We can try." She knew her voice sounded defensive. It felt odd to be standing here above him while he lay helpless in front of her.

"We need help," he argued. His voice became soft. "Enough games. Untie me and let me be on my way to Lyonsbridge so that we can see this thing settled."

"Nay."

His momentary look of irritation disappeared, replaced by a smile. "Ah, sweetheart, under any other circumstances I'd consider it an honor to be bound to your bed. Is this a typical cure you use for your patients?''

His reference to her nursing made her remember his wound with a flush of guilt. ''You're not feverish?'' she asked.

''Not from the head wound,'' he answered dryly.

She understood his remark exactly. She felt feverish herself. Taking a step back from the bed, she said, ''Then go to sleep.''

He wiggled his fingers inside their bindings. ''I don't think I can sleep like this.''

''I'll untie you if you promise not to try to leave.''

''Nay, that I can't do.''

''So be it.'' She pulled up her low stool to sit down, prepared to sit up awake until Francis came.

''You'd be more comfortable stretched out here on the bed,'' he said after a moment.

His voice was warm and coaxing. She looked away from him. ''There isn't room.''

''I'll move over.'' He turned his body sideways to make a narrow space on the cot beside him.

Bridget shook her head. She stared at the flicker of the candle, willing her racing pulse to slow. She had a feeling that it was going to be a long night.

Chapter Fourteen

Neither one had spoken for several moments when Ranulf moaned. The sound made Bridget jump. "What's wrong?" she asked, turning her head to look at him.

"Nay, 'tis nothing."

His eyes were closed and he appeared to be lying peacefully, but she thought she detected a slight sheen of moisture on his forehead. "Are you sure? Your head is not paining you?"

"Don't fret yourself about it."

She rose from the stool and walked over to him. It was hard to tell in the dim candlelight, but it seemed possible that his cheeks were flushed. "Is it aching?" she asked again.

He merely shook his head from side to side, but at the end of the motion, he gave another little moan. "It *is* hurting," she said in alarm. She sat down on the edge of the bed alongside him and put her hand against the cloth that still wrapped his head. "Let's see if the wound is warm."

"Perhaps more of me needs tending than my head, my little angel," he said in a husky voice. Then, before she knew what was happening, Ranulf sat up, easily breaking the ribbons from around both his hands and seized her in his arms. "Or should I say 'my little devil,' for tonight you're surely bent on mischief."

His quick move surprised her, but as he lifted her onto his lap, Bridget admitted that she had somehow known that the only way to keep Ranulf at St. Gabriel would be this. And she realized that it was what she'd been wanting since he'd first knocked on her door. Every one of her senses was racing with the wanting of it.

Nevertheless, she protested, "You broke my ribbons."

He chuckled and began kissing the edge of her ear. "I'll buy you new ribbons, sweetheart. And some stout rope for the next time you decide you need to take a captive."

"I didn't do a very good job of it."

He moved his kisses around to her mouth, settling her beside him on the bed. "Nay, you're wrong. For I've suddenly decided that an entire army of LeClerc's men couldn't make me leave for

Lyonsbridge just at this moment. You've got it your way, after all. I'm staying here.''

''I'm glad,'' she whispered, and raised her arms around his neck.

For several moments they kissed, focusing only on the interplay of their mouths. For the first time, Bridget was as much a participant as Ranulf, actively seeking to give him pleasure as well as receiving her own. She teased him with the tip of her tongue, then when he pulled back with a low groan, nipped gently at his lower lip. ''My angel has become a temptress,'' he murmured.

She gave a low laugh, then, daringly, slid her hand underneath his tunic and stroked his wool hose just where his body had hardened. ''She's had a good teacher,'' she whispered back.

He dropped his head back, shut his eyes and let her hand explore for a long moment, then finally, with a kind of growl, he lifted her to one side and stood to rid himself of his clothes. She followed his example and soon they tumbled back to the cot, both naked.

She stretched out like a cat, unconsciously seductive, and his eyes flared as he looked down at her. He ran his hand across her soft shoulder, then along the alabaster smoothness of her side and over the gentle curve of her hip. ''Mayhap 'tis time for the next lesson,'' he said in a choked voice.

She nodded, her throat too full to speak.

"Turn over," he told her.

Surprised, she did as he asked, rolling onto her stomach, and then his big hands were on her, moving up and down her back and up her neck, massaging gently while he gave a low murmur of admiration. His attentions moved to her bottom and the upper part of her thighs and finally down to her feet. Bridget felt as if she were floating on a sea of feeling.

His thumbs made circles on the soles of her feet, then she could feel his mouth on them and a delicate touch of tongue. She giggled a little as the caress caused a tickling sensation.

"Ah, laugh at me, will you?" he teased, straightening up to give her bottom a soft swat. "Then 'tis time we went to more serious business." He turned her and slid himself on top of her. "Would you like something more serious, sweetheart?" he asked low in her ear. At the same time he reached a hand out to feel that she was moist and ready for him.

"Aye, please," she whispered as she moved beneath him to make the fit of their bodies more perfect. He entered her swiftly, then stopped while each took a moment to savor the joining. It felt almost like relief, Bridget thought with wonder, as if she'd been waiting to recapture this feeling of completeness.

"Angel," Ranulf groaned, "I'm sorry—I have to—" He began to move inside her and there was a pent-up intensity to him that went beyond their first encounter. He seemed less focused on her, more into his own need. The thought made her feel sensual and powerful. She smiled as she gave herself up to the sensation of his strong, rhythmic strokes. In just moments, he gripped her more tightly and took her mouth in a fierce kiss as they reached a mutual climax.

The kiss subsided to tenderness, then became playful. "Ah, sweetling, that'll teach you to be holding strange men prisoner in your very own bedchamber," he said with a rueful laugh.

She grinned at him. "Mayhap 'twas exactly my intention."

He shook his head and rolled to collapse beside her. "I've never met a lady like you, Bridget. Part angel, part nurse, part chatelaine, part scholar and *all*—" he lifted up to plant a kiss on her cheek and lowered his voice "—all woman."

He undoubtedly meant the words to be complimentary, but Bridget felt as if a shadow had flickered across her glow of happiness. None of the qualities Ranulf had listed would alter the fact that she was a girl with no name raised by monks, while he was a nobleman. No matter how perfectly their bodies responded to each other, they were from two different worlds, and their time together was destined to be short. In fact, this one night might be the end of it.

Resolutely she pushed away the wave of sadness. "How many times can people do that?" she asked him.

He opened his eyes wide in surprise. "Do...ah... what we just did?"

"Aye. Can it be done more than once in an evening?"

Ranulf looked as if he was trying not to laugh at her earnest question. "Aye, sweetheart. So I've been told."

"Then I think we should."

"Should...ah—"

She gave a firm nod. "Do it one more time. At least once more, maybe twice. What do you think?"

This time Ranulf did not restrain his laugh. He put his arm around her and scooped her over on top of him. Under her stomach she could feel his manhood spring instantly to life. "Like I said before," he said with a grin, "I never turn down an angel."

Bridget came sleepily awake as once again she heard the unaccustomed sound of tapping on her door. She lay, still naked, entwined in Ranulf's arms. The candle had sputtered out and it was almost totally dark in the room, but she could feel from his sudden tensing that Ranulf had awakened, also.

He was quicker to act than she. Rising from the bed, he began groping in the dark for his clothes and handing her own garments to her. "Do you know who it is?" he whispered.

"Nay," she said, dressing hastily. "No one ever disturbs me here, especially not at night."

"Damnation," Ranulf swore. "My weapons are all over in my own room."

"I still have the spear point."

He chuckled. "I don't want to hurt your feelings, sweetheart, but you and your spear point are about as fierce as a ewe on lambing day."

Bridget gave an indignant huff. "I managed to subdue you," she said.

He leaned toward her in the darkness and planted a kiss that landed on her nose. "Aye, angel, that you did."

She had no time to question the laughter in his voice, since the tapping had grown more insistent. "Who is it?" she called.

"Open the door, Bridget," a voice replied.

"I think it's Brother Cyril," she said, surprised.

What on earth would he be doing here in the middle of the night?

She opened the door, flooding the room with moonlight. Cyril stood just outside, his chest heaving with exertion. He was half carrying Francis, who had begun to droop at his side.

Bridget gave a little cry, and Ranulf stepped around her to help Cyril support his brother monk. "What happened?" he asked.

Cyril, gasping, said merely, "He's been knifed."

Together the two men led the wounded monk into the little room and eased him down on the bed. Bridget had found the flint and another candle and set it in place. When the light flickered, she sank to her knees beside Francis and reached for his hand. "Where are you hurt, Francis?" she asked.

His eyes opened. "'Tis nothing, child. A little nick in the side, but the walk back proved a bit longer than I'd thought. I'm afraid I was quite a load for Cyril here the last few hundred yards."

"Were you at the work shed?" she asked, looking up at Cyril. The monk nodded, his face etched with guilt.

"Have they followed you here?" Ranulf asked, looking out the open door.

"Nay, Guise thinks he killed Francis. He left him for me to bury."

"'Twas the sheriff, then?" Ranulf confirmed.

"Aye."

"We can ask questions later," Bridget said. "First we must tend to your wound. Where are you hurt, Brother?"

Francis was holding his hand at his side. "I'm afraid I've ruined another habit, lass. More sewing for you."

Bridget choked back a tear. "I don't care about the habit, Francis. How bad is it?"

"Just a nick," he said again. Then his head slumped to one side in a faint.

"Blessed Mary," Bridget breathed. But putting a hand on his chest, she could feel that his heart beat strongly. She turned to the two men. "I'll need your help to get this habit off him so I can bind the wound."

The three set to work tending to the wounded monk with little talking. Bridget was reassured to see that Francis had spoken the truth. The knife had only put a gash along the edge of the monk's sizable belly, but the wound continued to bleed, and she decided that the best course would be simply to sew it up. Blessedly, Francis did not regain consciousness during the procedure.

When she was finished and had checked that he was breathing evenly and that the color of his face was normal, she sat back on her little stool with a sigh of relief.

"Now," she said, looking over at Cyril, who was standing miserably in the corner of the room, "tell us what happened."

The monk didn't try to soften the truth. He admitted his involvement with the sheriff and the baron.

"I thought that Alois would never allow us to bring the black metal to the world," he told them. "He was always so stern whenever I talked about sharing our discoveries, even with the people of Beauville." As usual, his black eyes snapped with energy when he spoke of his inventions, but this time they also held anguish.

Though Cyril had always been good to her, Bridget was not yet ready to forgive him. His actions had brought them to this. He'd nearly caused Francis's death and had put the future of St. Gabriel in real jeopardy. "How did the sheriff find out about the metal in the first place?" she asked coldly.

He looked down at the floor. "I brought it to him. I knew it would have many uses, and I thought he would be the logical one in town to talk with."

"And he went with it to the Baron of Darmaux?" Ranulf asked.

Cyril nodded. Then a sudden thought struck him. "I almost forgot. I must tell you, Sir Ranulf. It's about your brother."

Ranulf seemed to freeze. He waited, unblinking, while the monk continued, "They have him—LeClerc and Guise."

"He's alive?" Bridget asked, excited.

"Aye, but perhaps not for long. Tonight the sheriff said that he means to kill both the English brothers."

Ranulf's voice was barely recognizable. "Where is he?"

"They've had him prisoner in Mordin Castle. He was asking questions in a neighboring town about the black metal and the baron had him captured. He kept him alive to hold for ransom after—" Cyril paused with another flush of guilt "—after the black metal becomes known. But now he's given orders to kill him."

"How far is Mordin Castle?" Ranulf asked.

"I think it's about a two hours' ride east."

Ranulf's eyes glittered like blue ice. "How soon is the sheriff planning this *execution?*"

Cyril looked uncomfortable. "I—I don't know, milord. I'm afraid 'twas to be soon. I'm sorry to tell you that he spoke almost as if it was already done."

"Will you ride to Lyonsbridge?" Bridget asked, now feeling guilty for having tried to delay him.

"I don't think there's time." Again his voice sounded unnatural.

"You can't go up against LeClerc all by yourself," she said.

"The castle will be well guarded," Cyril added.

Ranulf rubbed his hands together. Just under the surface he seemed to be trying to control an immense anger. "Perhaps we could help," Bridget said in a weak voice.

"With your spear point?" Ranulf said with a note of disgust.

Cyril straightened up. "No, she's right. We could help—we monks."

Ranulf shook his head. "No thanks. I think I'd be better on my own than shepherding a group of—" He broke off his comment. "Forgive me," he said to Bridget. "Worry makes my tongue sharp."

Bridget nodded. "And it's completely understandable. But you should listen to Cyril. The monks may not be young warriors, but they are much more enterprising than you might think."

Ranulf's heart felt like someone had stuffed a boulder inside. Dragon was alive, only two hours' distance away, and he was in mortal danger, yet Ranulf might be unable to help him. He looked from Bridget's eager face back to Cyril. The idea of storming a castle with a band of monks was preposterous, but it appeared that he might have no other choice.

"Would they be willing to help me?" he asked.

"I know several who would," Cyril replied. "This is a dull place—a number of us have itched for an adventure for years."

"What if there's violence?" Ranulf asked.

Cyril smiled for the first time since he'd arrived with Francis. "I've been known to crack a head or two in my time before I saw the way of the Lord."

Very simply, it had been the most amazing evening of Ranulf's life. He shook his head as he looked around the bedraggled procession that made their way along the road to Mordin Castle. Leading the way were the six Courmier brothers. It had been Bridget's idea to ride to the dairy farm and see if the brothers would be willing to join their cause.

"If the other five are as brawny as Pierre," she told Ranulf, "you'd practically have an army right there."

Ranulf had had doubts that the family would be willing to take on such a risk for a perfect stranger, but agreed to have her ride to the farm with Ebert and ask. She suspected he had done it more than anything to keep her out of the way while he and the monks discussed battle strategy, but she went anyway, and rode back proudly followed by the six strapping dairymen and Jean the Smithy, as well.

"'Tis time someone went up against the baron,"

Pierre told Ranulf as he got off his mount, a dubious-looking plow horse. "It's common knowledge that he had Jean's brother killed, and, if my mother's memory is not fooling her, he may have been responsible for the death of your sweetheart's mother, the lady Charlotte."

Ranulf wasted little time in gratitude, but the handshake he gave the farmer was heartfelt.

He'd been surprised to see Jean. "You work for the baron," he pointed out.

"No longer," the smithy told him. "It's like Pierre said. 'Tis past time to stop him. I've been a coward long enough, but I'll not stand by and see another man lose his brother the way I lost mine."

So the force had grown, with borrowed horses, some brought by Jean from the smithy, some recruited along the way. They picked the ten most fit monks. Cyril had insisted on being included, over Ranulf's misgivings.

"I may have a few tricks that will help you out," the monk said, "and I need to try to make up for all the trouble I've caused."

Brother Jacques was the youngest in the abbey, though he'd been there for the better part of two decades, and they'd sent him as a lookout to the work shed. He reported back that the sheriff's men had evidently finished their evening work and left.

After that, Cyril led a group of those monks who

were to accompany the expedition back to the work shed ''to pick up some useful items.''

''You wouldn't happen to have any of those black metal weapons lying around, would you?'' Ranulf asked.

When Cyril shook his head, Jean pulled a heavy bag from the back of his horse and said, ''Here are some of the arrowheads that were left at the smithy, but none of us has a bow.''

Cyril said, ''Bring them along. We'll take care of the bow.''

And so it had gone through the frantic evening, until now, just before dawn, the group was assembled and on its way.

Jean's mount was the only other battleworthy horse. He dropped back to speak with Ranulf as it grew light. ''Do you think they'll post guard on the road?''

Ranulf shook his head. ''I don't know. Are you familiar with this area?''

Jean nodded. ''If there are guards, they'll be in the Venteux hills just to the west of the castle. I'll ride ahead and check them out if you like.''

Ranulf nodded, then said with his voice full. ''I won't forget this, my friend.''

Jean's face grew hard as he said, ''You owe me no thanks. I've waited eight years for this day.'' Then he whirled his horse and galloped up the road.

* * *

Bridget paced the length of the barn for the dozenth time. She should go work, she thought—weed the garden, bake some bread—but her thoughts were on the road to Mordin Castle. She'd asked Ranulf to take her along, but even she had to admit that the idea had been impractical. Her riding skills were still weak and she'd have slowed him down even more than the monks.

She smiled as she remembered how they'd looked setting off on Snail and Tortoise and assorted other borrowed animals, both horses and mules. The Courmier brothers had even brought along a donkey, which had been recruited to carry some of the equipment Brother Cyril had wanted to take along.

Most of the St. Gabriel monks had never done anything even remotely similar, and for those few who had once been soldiers, their days in the field had receded into dim memory. Worry fluttered at her stomach as she continued to pace.

The question of her own identity seemed to have faded in importance with the more urgent matter of Ranulf's brother, but as she thought about it, she realized that the events were connected. If she really were a LeClerc, then it was her relative who held Ranulf's brother. And, if what the old dairy woman remembered was true, it was the same relative who had pursued her mother and perhaps hounded her to her death.

She couldn't help thinking that the truth about her identity must be somewhere in the books that Abbot Josef had left to Brother Alois. Brother Alois kept them closely guarded in his own little office at the back of the library.

A thought struck her. Alois had declared that the monks should spend the day inside the church praying for the safety of their brethren. The rest of the abbey was deserted, including the abbot's office. Bridget looked over at one of the two milk cows who stood in its stall, chewing placidly.

"What do you think?" she asked the animal. "Do I dare?" The cow just watched her with its big brown eyes. "You're right," Bridget said with sudden decision. "I've been indifferent long enough. If we want things to happen in this life, we have to make them happen."

Then she marched out of the barn and headed in the direction of the abbot's office.

Chapter Fifteen

Mordin Castle was a small complex surrounding an old stone tower keep. The walls around it were crumbling, and it was apparent that little investment had been made in its upkeep over the years.

The party from St. Gabriel stopped on a small hill to survey the landscape. Jean had reported no guards along the way, and there were none in evidence at the front gate. The blacksmith had once again pulled his horse next to Ranulf. "Do you intend to ride right up and storm the place?" he asked.

Ranulf shook his head. "We can't risk that. They might be able to do some harm to my brother before we can get to him." That is, if he was still alive, Ranulf added to himself, which was the question that had tortured him with every pound of Thunder's hooves all the way from the abbey. He was so close, it was unbearable to think that he might lose Dragon now.

"What are we going to do?" Pierre Courmier had ridden up and heard Ranulf's answer.

Ranulf gave a grim smile. "The monks and I have worked out a strategy." He pointed to a grove of trees. "We'll stop over there and make the final plans."

Except for Ebert and Jacques, the monks dismounted stiffly, unused to the long ride, but Ranulf gave them little time to nurse their soreness. Calling the group all together, he quickly mapped out the plan. They assumed that Edmund Brand was being held in some kind of basement dungeon. The task before them was to enter the castle, subdue the guards, find and release the prisoner and escape before harm could come to any of them.

"Count me in for dealing with the guards," Jean said, clapping his huge hands together. The Courmier brothers nodded agreement.

"Good," Ranulf said. "But first we have a change of costume for you all." He nodded to Ebert and Cyril, who pulled a big bundle off the back of the donkey and unrolled it on the ground. It was full of white robes.

"Oh, no," Jean protested. "I'm not dressing like an old lady." When several of the monks gave him admonishing looks, he amended his objection to,

"That is, it doesn't seem right, trying to be holy-like."

Cyril picked up one of the habits and tossed it at the smithy. "Overcome your scruples just this once, my son. 'Tis for a good cause."

There was no more protest as the Courmiers, Ranulf and Jean donned the robes. They came to mid-calf on the tall men, but when one surveyed the group as a whole, the impression was of a band of wandering brothers.

Quickly Ranulf outlined the rest of the plan, then they mounted up and set off down the hill toward the castle. The sun's first rays were already striking its eastern wall.

As they had anticipated, a sleepy guard threw open the door and let them inside without question. "The baron's not here, brothers," he told them, "but I warrant you may take some refreshment in the great hall."

"Peace be with you, my son," Ebert said, and they steered their horses across the bailey toward the keep.

Ranulf's hopes rose. Perhaps no one would challenge them and they would be able to rescue Dragon peacefully.

They got as far as the big wooden doors of the tower. There they were met by a dour-faced guard who barked, "We'll bring some porridge out to the courtyard. Then you must be about your journey."

Ebert stepped up to the man and said, "We'd take shelter inside, my son."

The guard shook his head. "Nay, no one's allowed inside Mordin Castle when the baron's away."

Ebert looked back at Ranulf, who shrugged and said, "Let the choice be on his head, Brother."

In an instant, the place was in chaos. Ranulf, the Courmiers and the blacksmith threw off their cumbersome robes. Ranulf drew his sword and the others pulled out various weapons the blacksmith had brought for them. Instantly, over a dozen guards appeared from inside the keep, most brandishing short swords.

From underneath the monks' robes appeared a variety of mysterious instruments. Cyril had an apparatus that looked like a slingshot, but used a narrow slot into which he could fit the black metal arrowheads that he carried in a burlap sack over his shoulder.

Brother Jacques had some kind of lever rigged to a spring that when it was pulled one way, shot the opposite with tremendous force. He used it against the chin of an oncoming guard and the man sank to the ground, out cold. Jacques looked around, surprised and a little embarrassed at his own success. When he saw that no one had paid attention to his deed, he ran over to another guard and repeated the performance.

The guard who had refused to admit them had engaged Ranulf with a broad sword, but the man was a poor match for the English knight and Ranulf had soon laid him flat with a blow to the side of his head. Within minutes, every one of the Mordin guards lay unconscious on the ground or had slunk away to the back part of the castle to nurse wounds. None of the men from St. Gabriel had more than a scratch.

Ranulf looked around his crew with a whistle of amazement. "If we'd had you lads in the Holy Lands, they'd be Christian now," he said.

The men exchanged grins of triumph, but Ebert looked around at the men on the ground and said, "We didn't kill any, did we? I'm virtually certain *that* would not be allowed by the Rule."

"It's a bit late to be worried about that, Brother Ebert," said Brother Jacques. "But, nay, none of these men appear to be dead."

"Now we just need to find my brother," Ranulf told them. His heart had started to race at the prospect. Was it possible that Dragon was here, perhaps just underneath where he stood now in the castle entry? Then the fingers of fear crept up his throat once more. What if they were too late?

Jean seemed to recognize his emotion. Speaking in a voice of authority, he told the men, ''We need to split up and go to different parts of the castle, searching each room. If you find the prisoner, shout and bring him back here.''

Ranulf regained his voice. ''Go in groups of three or four in case you encounter more opposition. And hurry, before these men start regaining consciousness.''

Jean and two of the Courmier brothers headed up the winding stairway to the upper floors. The other dairymen went back out into the courtyard to be sure the complex was secure. Ebert and Cyril followed Ranulf down the stairs to the lower level.

The stairs grew blacker the farther they went. Ranulf lifted a torch from a wall bracket. The stairs ended at what appeared to be a solid wall of stone. He turned around and looked at the two monks with an expression of bewilderment. ''We've reached a dead end, it appears,'' he said.

Cyril and Ebert were both looking intently at the wall. ''I don't think so,'' Cyril said.

Ranulf waited while the two monks bent and stretched to study each stone. Finally Cyril straightened up with a smile of triumph. '''Tis an old system of counterlevers,'' he said. Then he leaned heavily on the rock he had chosen and the entire wall started to turn into a huge door.

Ranulf's palms began to sweat in anticipation, but when the wall opened, it revealed a small chamber, and it was empty. He nearly cried out with the disappointment.

Ebert took the torch from his numb fingers and lifted it high to see into the little room. "There," he said, pointing. On the other side of the chamber was another small door. From behind it they could hear distinct rustling sounds.

With a sudden surge of energy, Ranulf ran to the door and tugged at the handle. It wouldn't budge. "Dragon!" he called, his voice desperate. From behind the door they could hear an answering human voice. "Dragon!" he yelled again, then yanked on the handle furiously again and again, until Cyril put a hand on his arm.

"Let me try, Sir Ranulf," he said. "The door is locked." He held some kind of tool, which he inserted into a slit just beneath the door handle. Ranulf and Ebert waited in tense silence while he worked.

After several moments, Cyril let out a long sigh. "That should do it, I think." He stepped back and gestured for Ranulf to try the door again.

Ranulf reached out and pulled the handle. The door opened with a harsh rasp against the stone floor, and there standing on the other side, looking pale but fit, was Dragon.

The two brothers stared at each other for a long moment, then fell into an embrace. When he could finally speak, Ranulf stepped back and said, "You were ever one to get yourself in trouble, little brother."

Edmund grinned. "That's because I knew I could count on my big brothers to get me out of it."

Ranulf shook his head. "Next time don't be so damned sure of that. I've better things to do with my life than chase you around the world."

Edmund looked from Ranulf to the two monks. "Not—er—not following the example of these good brothers, I hope."

"Nay, you lout. These are two of the White Monks of St. Gabriel. They've come to help me save your miserable hide."

"St. Gabriel? 'Tis the abbey where I was heading to try to find the—"

"The black metal, aye. But if you don't mind, brother, the explanations can wait until we're safely out of this place. Are you all right? You can ride?"

"Aye, my jailers have not been bad folks. They've kept me fed and well. But, God Almighty, it's good to see you, Ran."

"And you."

Their gazes held one more time, then they all turned to make their way up the dark stairs.

* * *

One of the paramount instructions of the Rule was obedience in all things, and Bridget felt more than a little guilty stepping into Alois's office, which had always been strictly forbidden to her. But now that she had started the search for her name, the nagging wouldn't stop, and the opportunity seemed too good to pass up.

The room was mainly occupied with the abbot's big writing table, a duplicate of the ones in the illumination room next to the library. Before they had become engrossed in their inventions, the monks of St. Gabriel, just like their fellow orders all over Europe, had spent long hours copying manuscripts. The writing table was clean, but Bridget knew that the abbey records were usually kept in a chest along one wall of the sparsely furnished room.

She walked across to the big wooden box and sank down beside it. The lid was heavy, and just for a moment as she opened it, she wondered if she should slam it shut again and walk away. If this box held the key to her family and her past, perhaps she didn't want to see what was inside.

She didn't have to look. She could remain in ignorance—stay simply Bridget, the no-name girl known only to the monks and hidden away from the rest of the world. Once she knew who she really was, it could change everything.

She hesitated a moment longer, then took a deep breath and pulled it open. Inside, the neat stacks of books gave no indication of any ominous meaning they might have for her life.

She lifted the top volume, brought it over to the writing table and perched on the stool to read. The book was a record of abbey accounts and important events, feast days and market purchases. Bridget felt a stab of disappointment. If this was all these books contained, she couldn't see how they could give her the answers she sought.

It was growing close to midday, and soon the monks would be breaking their prayers for the daily meal. What she needed to do was find the book that corresponded to the time of her birth, twenty-two years ago. She knelt once again beside the chest and began to search more quickly. She found it in the seventh volume she searched—Anno Domini 1173.

Her anticipation had built the longer she looked, and she couldn't help a small cry of disappointment when she opened the book and found nothing but the same kind of daily records that had been in the others.

She sat on the floor next to the chest, the big volume in her lap and forced herself to read. If nothing else, she'd learn some interesting things about what St. Gabriel was like before she'd been a part of it. It wasn't what she'd come to find out, but it was something.

She'd skipped through the early pages, which were similar to the other volumes, and started into the main record when a piece of parchment slipped out of the middle and fell to the floor. She could see immediately that it was written in French, not Latin. She reached over to retrieve it, her fingers suddenly shaky.

The signature at the bottom was Henri LeClerc, Baron of Darmaux.

Biting down hard on her bottom lip, Bridget started to read.

She never heard the door to the office open, and it was a moment before Alois's soft voice broke her concentration. "Somehow I always knew that we wouldn't be able to keep you in peaceful ignorance your whole life." His voice was full of regret.

Bridget gave a guilty jump and slammed the book shut. Then she recovered and met Alois's gaze. "It never seemed to matter," she said. "I've been happy here."

He stepped into the room. "Aye. We all have, and now it's beginning to come apart. Cursed be on Cyril and his devil's inventions. I knew from the beginning that it would mean the end of St. Gabriel.''

Alois had an expression on his face that Bridget had never seen before. His normally cold eyes had an unnatural glow. "Surely not, Brother Alois," she protested. "Once Ranulf and the monks deal with the problem of the black metal—"

"Aye, the black metal," Alois interrupted. "It makes men greedy and causes them to break promises and want more."

She was having difficulty understanding him, and it frightened her. Alois, the serene leader who always took such calm control, now seemed nearly incoherent. It almost made her forget the paper she'd just been reading, but not entirely.

She picked it up. "You knew about this bargain?" she asked Alois.

"That the monks of St. Gabriel would keep you secret forever in return for your life? Aye."

"But why?"

Alois looked down at her with an odd smile. "You were such a sweet little thing, Bridget. None of us had ever seen anything quite like you when your mother gave you birth. We couldn't bear the thought of giving you into the hands of the baron. He would have killed you back then. I'm certain of it."

"My mother was his cousin."

"Aye, and the true heir to Darmaux. Henri was to inherit only Mordin, a much lesser estate. It wasn't enough for him."

"So he forced her to run away."

"Once he discovered she was with child, another possible heir, he became enraged. She refused to name the father, and he was certain that it was some powerful knight who would come to help her enforce her claim."

Her father. The scrap of parchment had given no clue. "Who was my father?" she asked. Everything inside her had gone very still.

"Ah, there was the irony." Alois gave a hollow laugh. "Your father was no landowning knight, Bridget. In fact, he never would have been able to give you a legitimate name."

"Will you tell me who he was?"

"'Tis no longer of any importance. Nothing is, really." Alois walked toward her. "This is the end of it, you know. It started with that Englishman's arrival. Now the black metal is known and your secret as well. It's the end of all of it."

Bridget was growing alarmed. She'd never seen Alois like this before and the odd look in his eyes was scaring her. "Forgive me, Brother, but you're wrong. St. Gabriel is as strong as ever. Once Ranulf finds his brother, everything will go back to the way it was...."

Alois was shaking his head as he drew slowly nearer. "Nay, little Bridget, it's too late to put things to right. St. Gabriel is dead and the rest of us will soon follow."

Then she looked up in horror as he lifted an inkstand from his writing table and sent it crashing down on her head.

Alois stood, head bowed, hands tucked into the sleeves of his habit. "'Twas the girl herself who discovered the secret, milord. No one at the abbey revealed anything to her."

The abbot had been forced to walk to Darmaux Castle since both the mules had been taken for the expedition to Mordin. He'd found the baron in a furious temper, shouting at the sheriff, Guise, who knelt before him on the hard stone floor of the castle entryway. A messenger had just ridden in from Mordin Castle to report the escape of the English prisoner.

Alois knew that it wasn't a good moment to arrive with his own news, but he was beyond caring. For too many years he'd felt the burden of his pact with the devil. Now it was time to start on his way to hell and begin to enjoy his eternity of paying for the fruits of his bargain.

"Our bargain was that I wouldn't use my power with the bishop to take over St. Gabriel lands as long as you kept the girl quiet," LeClerc pointed out. "If she surfaces and finds support, she could still lay claim to the Darmaux holdings. And that, my fine abbot, is not going to happen."

"Do what you will with her, milord," Alois said, lifting his head to meet the baron's violet gaze with indifference. "I've left her tied in the work shed."

"And before long the Englishman will be back there with whatever army it was he mustered to storm Mordin," LeClerc screamed. Rage made the veins pop on each side of his neck. He kicked at the sheriff, who still knelt before him. "Assemble the men, you incompetent fool. This time I'll go with you to be sure the job's done right. I want the girl dead and the abbey secure, and I want the English brothers recaptured and killed before the sun sets on this day."

For the first few moments, Bridget wondered if there might not be some truth to Alois's words. It did seem as if the world she had known was dead, or at least dying. First there had been the shock over Brother Cyril's betrayal, then the revelation that the monks had cared for her all these years not for her own sake, but to protect the abbey. Now Brother Alois. He'd been eerily detached as he'd forced her to the work shed and left her there in a dark corner behind a cupboard, and with each move

Bridget's conviction grew that the abbot's mind had become unhinged.

"Poor little Bridget, poor little Bridget," he'd said over and over while tying her hands and feet as if she'd been a calf bound for market. "I tried to protect you, but now it's over. I must go to the baron, and we'll see what he wants to do with you."

Then he'd left her, and for the first few minutes she lay quiet, trying to sort out the events of the past couple of days. According to Brother Josef's agreement with the baron, the abbey would be allowed to raise the female child of Charlotte LeClerc in secret on the condition that the child never be made aware of her connection to the LeClerc family. In exchange, the baron would use his power to ensure that the all-powerful bishopric would leave the abbey of St. Gabriel alone to function in peace and autonomy. The devil's bargain threatened to color everything Bridget had ever believed about her upbringing.

It was the ropes biting into the sensitive skin of her wrists that reminded her that she couldn't afford the luxury of thinking just now. Before long, Alois would have reached the baron, and, if he was as ruthless as she suspected, LeClerc might be here soon with some of his men, ready to rid himself of a potentially dangerous relative.

With the day designated for prayers, it was unlikely that any of the monks would be visiting the
work shed, which meant that if she was to get free,
she'd have to figure out how to do it herself. Slowly
she inched her way out from behind the cupboard.
Once she started, she discovered that it wasn't too
difficult to crawl along the floor, but it was terribly
slow. She'd never get far this way.

She lifted her head and looked around the room.
With all the various apparatus the monks used for
their tinkering, there surely must be something she
could use to cut the ropes. It took her only a minute
to spot the solution, and it turned out to be a discarded piece of the black metal itself. She used it
first to saw away at the rope binding her feet. Then,
with more difficulty, she held it in her mouth and
worked it against the rope at her wrists. The process
seemed endless, and her neck ached with the effort,
but finally the strands of the thick cord started un-
raveling and then broke apart.

She was free, but now what? she thought. It
could be hours yet before Ranulf and the others
returned from Mordin Castle. What if Alois returned with the baron's men in the meantime? She
thought about going back to the church to talk to
the other monks about Alois's perfidy, but rejected
the idea almost immediately. The monks who were
left behind at the abbey were the older ones. Many

of them were now frail. It would serve no purpose to alarm them and get them ready to fight a battle with a well-armed force such as the baron's men.

She stood for a moment in the center of the work shed, thinking. No, if the baron's men came back here looking for her, she had to be ready for them herself. Slowly she turned in a circle, looking around at the monks' tinkerings. It always amazed her that while some of their inventions had proven useful around the abbey, many more had much less peaceful intentions.

It seemed to be the way with men, she thought with a sigh. If she had an army of her own inside this room, she undoubtedly could face the baron and his men in a standoff, just with the materials right here. But she had no army. She turned in a circle until her gaze lit on the blast fire that was roaring away as usual.

She had no army, she thought with sudden resolve. But she had a plan.

Chapter Sixteen

There was still much to be settled, Ranulf thought to himself as they made their way back to St. Gabriel. There would be a reckoning with LeClerc. And the mystery of Bridget's heritage. Then there was the black metal. Now that the secret was known to so many, would war-hungry overlords start to build blast fires across Europe to produce arrows and lances that could pierce any armor? Was this what the world called progress?

But as he rode alongside Dragon in the bright Normandy sunlight, it seemed to him that his own world had been once again set to rights. Every now and then he looked over at his brother's face, so like his own, to reassure himself that it was really true that he was safe and whole and that they were together again.

"So what's she like, this Bridget of yours?" Edmund asked, interrupting his thoughts.

"First of all, she's not *my* Bridget."

"Nay, which is why she was the first thing you spoke of when we left Mordin Castle."

"I was merely curious what you would think of her."

Edmund grinned at his brother. "If she's as bonny as you say, I might think a great deal more of her than you want me to."

"What about Diana, you lout? Have you forgotten your affianced bride?"

Edmund sat back in the saddle of his sway-backed mount with a sigh. "Nay, but it's been so long, I feel almost as if Diana is some kind of dream."

"She's no dream, but a flesh-and-blood woman who's waited for you these three years past. More than a wandering rogue like you deserves, I should say."

Edmund nodded. "Aye," he said softly. Then he straightened up with another grin. "But having a bride back home doesn't pluck the eyes from a man's body. Come on, Ran, you're talking to a man who's spent five months in a dark prison. Is she comely? Is her hair fair or dark? Is she deliciously plump with nicely curving hips and full—"

He broke off as his brother leaned over in his saddle to give him a swat. "I ought to have left you to rot," Ranulf said with affection.

Edmund eyed his brother with a smile of sympathy. "But, nevertheless, she's not *your* Bridget."

"Nay, she's not."

Edmund grinned more broadly, and the two spurred their mounts to catch up with the others.

In the end she had had to recruit Francis. Her preparations went smoothly, but the operation would require two people, one to give the signal that the baron's men were approaching and one to light the fire in the auxiliary furnace. The timing had to be perfect, because if she waited too long, the baron's men might have entered the work shed before the auxiliary furnace had time to heat up. This would put them directly in the line of the explosion.

Bridget didn't want anyone to be hurt. She simply wanted the blast to scare the baron away, and, in the process, destroy the hated source of much of their trouble. The monks would be disappointed over the loss of their tinkerings, but they'd soon discover ways to invent new ones.

Francis was sore, but moving well in spite of his wound. He'd been horrified to hear about Alois. "Who'd have ever thought?" he asked her. "He's led us all these many years."

Bridget didn't have time to dwell on the revelations of the day. She had an army to fend off and a furnace to blow up.

They'd agreed that Francis would station himself along the edge of the meadow that led to the abbey. When he caught sight of the sheriff, the baron or any of his men, he'd give a signal on a shrill whistle that Brother Jacques had invented for calling in brothers who were working out in the fields.

Bridget busied herself stuffing the little auxiliary furnace with all the wood shavings and kindling she could find—anything that would burn fast and hot. Then she settled down by the blast fire to wait.

Dusk was gathering outside the two big work shed windows by the time Francis's whistle finally sounded. Bridget had almost become convinced that the baron had decided to wait until his men's usual nighttime work visit to deal with her, but the high-pitched sound was unmistakable.

Hands shaking, she started to strike the flint. In her nervousness, it took her several tries before the sparks ignited the dry wood, but once the fire took, it flared quickly. She looked around the work shed with a sudden pang of remorse. Perhaps there were things here that she should have removed, things the monks might value. Well, it was too late now, she decided with a shrug, as the little furnace fire turned into a regular blaze. In any event, the Rule forbade becoming attached to material goods. Nevertheless, on a sudden impulse, she slipped the piece of the black metal she'd used to cut her ropes into the little purse that Ranulf had bought for her the day in the market.

An ominous rumbling from inside the blast fire reminded her that if she didn't move quickly, the entire building could explode with her inside of it. Quickly she ran out the big front doors and into the woods. She looked back at the shed just once with a final little prayer that her timing would work out as she had planned. She wanted the thing done, but she didn't want anyone harmed.

She'd only made it a few hundred yards when all at once it seemed as if the woods around her were full of men. Whirling around, she sought to hide herself behind a narrow ash tree, but within moments, she was seized by a man wearing some kind of special livery.

"I've got her," the man yelled. "Over here." He held her easily, though she did her best to kick and squirm her way out of his grasp. "Hold still, you little savage," the man barked, then he threw her over his shoulder and carried her that way through the trees as she beat with her fists on his back.

They arrived at the clearing in front of the work shed and he dumped her unceremoniously on the ground. "She's a hellcat, that one," the man said, rubbing his neck where she'd clawed at him.

She looked from where she lay sprawled in the dust into the face of a richly dressed man who stood snapping a riding whip at his side. The man spoke to her captor. "'Tis the kind of opponent you can handle, my dear sheriff—a woman."

The face of the man who had seized her darkened, but he remained silent.

"They spoke the truth," the man said to her. "You are the very image of my late, lamented cousin."

Bridget was relieved that she saw no family resemblance in the face of this cruel-eyed man. "The cousin whose lands you stole?" she asked.

The baron smiled. "Aye, you are like her. She, too, never knew when to keep her mouth shut." He turned to the sheriff and said, "Kill her."

At that moment there was a sudden rush of noise from inside the work shed and Bridget realized with panic that the auxiliary furnace had begun forcing air into the main blast fire. She looked around the clearing. They were too close. If the furnace exploded now, they'd all be killed.

"Wait," she said as the sheriff drew a long dagger from his belt. "Everyone must get back from here—it's dangerous." A roar from the blast fire reinforced her words.

The baron's head went up. "She's done something to the furnace. Guise, take these men and go find out what's wrong," he said, gesturing to three guards who were standing nearby.

Guise looked from the guards to the baron, then to Bridget. The furnace gave another bellow. "Go in yourself, LeClerc," he said. "I'm not going to get myself blown up for your sake."

The baron's face screwed up in a rage. "I order you to go in, Guise!"

The sheriff took a step back and sheathed his knife. "I'd suggest we do what the girl says and get out of here."

"You bloody fool!" the baron shouted. Then he turned to the three men, said, "Follow me," and started inside the work shed.

"Stop him," Bridget pleaded, but the sheriff merely stood, his expression hard, and watched as the baron disappeared inside.

The furnace's rumblings grew heavier and several of the guards took off running into the woods. The sheriff stood without moving as Bridget got to her feet. "We all need to leave," she said again.

Guise nodded but didn't move.

"Come on," she yelled. Then the ground beneath her feet shook with a tremendous blast.

It was already dusk by the time the weary procession returning from Mordin Castle reached the fork in the road where Ranulf had once stopped to kiss Bridget. They'd been up all night and riding the entire day. Ranulf's head was throbbing, and he could tell that Dragon was feeling the unaccustomed exertion after months of idleness.

"It will be good to get back to the abbey," he told his brother. "'Tis a peaceful place."

"I never figured you for the monastical life, brother," Edmund said.

"Nay, 'tis not the lifestyle I'd choose, but I'm ready to sleep the sun around in one of their beds."

"What about the baron and the sheriff?" Ranulf had related the entire tale to his brother during the course of the ride.

"They'll have to be dealt with, but now that you're with me, I'm in no hurry. We can ride to Lyonsbridge for help."

"And take your lady with us?"

Ranulf was quiet for a moment. When he spoke, he did not bother to deny that Bridget was his lady. "Aye. I'll not leave her alone again."

"Grandmother will love her."

"That she will. She's already taken to Thomas's wife, Alyce Rose, as if she were her own granddaughter."

"Grandmother always said there were too many lads in the household," Edmund said with a fond smile of remembrance. "I can't wait to see her."

"She'll have a word or two to say to you for scaring us all like you did."

"I warrant she will," Edmund said ruefully. "But when I tell them 'twas King Richard himself who sent me to search for the mysterious black metal that was starting to appear around the continent in jousting tournaments, perhaps they'll forgive me."

"I believe Grandmother would forgive you if you were working for the devil himself, however—"

His words were interrupted by the distant sound of a blast. Ranulf stood up in his stirrups and looked in the direction of the abbey as an odd orange glow colored the twilight sky. "Bridget!" he cried, and spurred Thunder forward.

They'd left the monks far behind by the time they reached the meadow leading to St. Gabriel, but his brother, Jean and the Courmiers had managed to keep up. Ranulf had already guessed at the location and cause of the explosion and was not surprised to see armed men dressed in Darmaux livery fleeing in chaos.

"'Tis the baron," he shouted to Edmund. "I have to find Bridget."

One man was running toward the work shed instead of away. Ranulf instantly recognized the monk's round shape. "Francis!" he called.

The monk veered toward him, his chest heaving with exertion. "Bridget was at the work shed," he panted. "Hurry!" Then he continued running in the direction of the fire.

Ranulf felt a cold chill.

Edmund took a quick survey of the territory. "This work shed is over at the blast sight?" he asked. At Ranulf's nod, he said, "You and Jean head over there. Your dairymen and I will ride into the abbey compound itself and be sure that it's secure."

Ranulf nodded, momentarily unable to answer. From the looks of the sky, the entire work shed was going up in smoke. If Bridget had been inside...

"What do you want us to do with the baron if we capture him?" Edmund asked.

Ranulf forced himself to concentrate on the task at hand. "Just hold him. 'Tis for the French king to determine his fate. But the sheriff is mine," he added, pointing to his head. "I've a score to settle with him."

Edmund nodded and the brothers wasted no more time on words. Ranulf signaled to Jean, and the two left the road to cut through the woods in the shortest route to the work shed. Above the trees the eerie orange glow had grown bigger.

"'Tis the furnace," Jean said.

"Aye," Ranulf agreed.

"I hope there's nothing left of the cursed thing," the smithy said. Then they lapsed into silence.

Slowly Bridget picked herself up from the ground, amazed that all her limbs seemed to function properly. It took some time to register that her efforts with the blast furnace had actually succeeded. She'd blown the wicked device up. She straightened and rubbed her arms. Aye, she'd blown it up, but at what price?

With a sick feeling she turned to look at the doors through which the baron had disappeared moments before. The three guards he'd motioned to follow him lay sprawled on the ground in front of the door, but all appeared to be moving. There was no sign of the baron, and the inside of the work shed was an inferno.

Behind her, the sheriff was stirring. She started backing away as he reared up beside her, but he seized her shoulder with a big, meaty hand. "Oh no, you don't, you wretched wench," he said.

His fingers dug painfully into the side of her neck as she struggled to free herself. "I suppose I owe you a debt for this night," he said. "'Twas past time someone set that bastard LeClerc burning in the hell he deserves.'' In the supernatural glow of the fire, his face leered over her.

''Then let me be,'' she said.

He showed a mouth full of blackened teeth in a lopsided devil's grin. ''I believe I need to think of a proper way to show my gratitude.''

''You can show it to me instead, Guise.'' With a wave of relief, Bridget recognized Ranulf's voice. But her relief turned to worry as the sheriff shoved her to one side and turned to face the knight. Ranulf was a big man, but the sheriff was much bigger, and she could tell from Ranulf's face that he was once again in pain from his wound.

The sheriff smiled and drew his short sword. ''You won't slip away from me with any of your damned acrobatics this time, Englishman,'' he said. Then he lifted the sword over his head and brought it crashing down toward the knight. Ranulf jumped to avoid the blow.

Bridget glanced over to see that Jean was holding the three guards at bay, motioning with his sword for them to stay where they lay on the ground. She looked around for something she could use as a weapon to help Ranulf with the sheriff, but the clearing seemed bare of any large branches or rocks.

Ranulf had recovered his balance and drawn his

own sword, but he swayed as he slashed at Guise. The sheriff tried another death blow, and once again Ranulf managed to slip from underneath his onslaught. Bridget felt her pulse race as she watched them—the sheriff bearing down on Ranulf with huge, powerful strokes of his heavy sword and Ranulf parrying and dodging from side to side to escape them. Bridget could see that he was tiring. All color had drained from his face.

In desperation, she pulled the small piece of black metal from her purse. When the sheriff had his back to her, she leapt onto his back and scratched his neck with it. Guise gave a great bellow and let his sword clatter to the ground as he reached behind with both hands and grabbed her head to pull her off him, shaking her violently. "I'll break your neck, you little—" he began. Before he could finish, Ranulf had run him through with his sword.

His hands loosened their hold around Bridget, then, like a great tree, he toppled slowly to the ground.

Ranulf hardly gave him a glance as he dropped down to lift Bridget from where she'd fallen. "Are you all right, sweetheart?" he cried.

She lay back in his arms, suddenly exhausted, and whispered, "Aye."

Ranulf looked across the clearing to be sure that

Jean needed no help with the three guards. Then he looked over his shoulder at Guise. When Ranulf had seen the sheriff's big fingers move around Bridget's slender neck, he hadn't bothered to try anything with finesse. He'd simply lunged at the big man's chest, and from all appearances the blow had been lethal.

Turning back to Bridget, he lifted her tenderly so that her head was against his cheek. "You may have saved both our lives, my fierce angel," he told her.

She shook her head. "Is he——?"

"Aye, dead," Ranulf confirmed. "But what about the baron?"

She nodded weakly toward the still-burning building.

"Inside," she said.

Ranulf let out a long breath and said, "So be it."

"The baron was my mother's cousin," she said, struggling to sit up. "And, Ranulf, Alois has been in league with him. For years. And——"

"Shh, sweetheart," he said, rocking her in his arms. "We'll sort it all out in time. For now it's enough that I've found my brother and you're safe. Nothing else matters."

Chapter Seventeen

Bridget picked up another torn habit from the pile on the floor and stabbed her needle angrily into the thick linen. "I don't *want* Darmaux Castle or any of the rest of it," she said. "Everything I need is here inside the abbey." She gestured around the kitchen. "I don't hear you desirous of making any changes, Brother Francis."

Francis sat back on the bench with a sigh. "My course in life is set, child, and, aye, I'm content here now that Brother Alois has been removed and sent to Rome and Ebert has become abbot. But life has so much more to offer you. You're a noble-woman now, an heiress. You'd be a fine match for Ranulf, if that's what you should choose."

Bridget gave a little sniff of disdain. "I'm not a whit different than I was yesterday."

"Nay, but you have more money," Francis pointed out with a smile.

"I don't want it," she said again.

Francis tried another tack. "Bridget, now that everything has come out about the black metal and Alois's bargain, the bishopric has become involved in the operation of the abbey again. Soon we'll have one of the bishop's representatives moving in to check out our operation, perhaps even the bishop himself."

"Let them come. I'll just hide myself away like I've always done."

"There's been enough hiding at St. Gabriel," Francis said gravely. "I believe all this is the Lord's way of telling us to turn to more holy paths."

"Do you think the bishop will forbid the tinkerings?" she asked in alarm.

"Nay, though there will never be another blast fire at St. Gabriel."

"Nor anywhere else, I trust," Bridget added. "'Tis nothing that will make the world a better place."

"But things will be different here, Bridget. No more secrets. We can't hide you any longer, and it's time you took your rightful place in the world."

Bridget's eyes glistened as she looked over at the monk. "I don't want to leave, Francis. I warrant I've been a lot happier here than my cousin ever was with all his estates. My mother was right to run away from him.''

"But your mother was running away to the man she loved.''

Bridget's needle froze halfway to the next stitch. "To my father,'' she said slowly.

"Aye.''

She let her hands fall into her lap. "No more secrets, you said, Francis. Doesn't that mean that it's finally time for you to tell me about my father?''

Francis hesitated so long that Bridget thought that once again she'd be denied the knowledge she sought, but then he said slowly. "Your father was one of us, Bridget. He was one of the White Monks of St. Gabriel.''

The room seemed to move. She grasped the edge of the fireplace to keep her balance. "A monk?'' she gasped. "But he…he couldn't be. Monks can't—'' She faltered for the word. "How could he?'' she ended.

Francis's eyes were wise. "He could because, besides being a monk, he was a human being, just as we all are. When Charlotte began coming here to escape from her cousin's abuses, she and Brother Renault fell in love, just as young people have been falling in love since the beginning of time.''

"But the Rule…'' she stuttered. "The vows…''

"Aye, the Rule, the vows," Francis agreed. "Brother Renault suffered for his transgressions, but in the end, I think he knew that he had God's forgiveness."

"They were truly in love?" Bridget asked wistfully.

Francis nodded. "More than any two people I've ever known. He asked to be released from his vows, and in view of your mother's condition, Brother Josef gave him a dispensation and set him free. They were married the same day."

"They were *married?*" Bridget felt a flood of joy. Somehow she had always imagined that her parents had been star-crossed lovers who had never been able to swear to their love in any kind of ceremony.

"Aye. 'Twas here in the church. We all attended." Francis gave a dismissive wave of his hand. "Oh, I imagine the church itself would never have sanctioned any of it, but it didn't matter, because by that time we knew that your mother was dying, and Renault knew it, too."

For some reason she couldn't understand, she was afraid to ask the next question, but she forced herself. "What happened to him?"

Francis looked away. "You must understand, child. Renault knew that as a disgraced monk he would most likely not be allowed to raise you. One of his very last deeds was to ask the rest of us to care for you and keep you safe. He loved you very much. He agonized over leaving you, but he decided it would be the best thing for you.''

''And then what happened?'' she asked softly.

''And then he went to be with his Charlotte, for he said that there would never be a moment of joy in an earthly life without her.''

Bridget sat in silence for a long moment. Suicide was a mortal sin, even when the person no longer had a reason to live. Her father had died alone and unshriven. ''Do you think that they are together?'' she asked, her voice breaking.

''Aye, child, I do, for I believe in a loving God. He's the one who allowed your parents to love each other, and I can't believe that he gave them that gift only to take it away from them for eternity.''

She looked up, the tears rolling down her face, and reached for Francis's hand. ''Thank you,'' she said.

Francis sniffed back some tears of his own and gave her hand a squeeze. Then he let it go and sat back, since the touch was against the Rule.

Ranulf shook his head as Pierre offered the pitcher of ale to refill his mug. ''Nay, Dragon and I must be leaving,'' he said, ''but I thank you warmly for your hospitality and more than I can say for my brother's life."

He stood and pushed back his bench. The spacious main room of the Courmier farmhouse looked cramped with the two English knights, the six strapping Courmiers and the bulky blacksmith all crowded into it. Camille Courmier had given up and retired to her room.

Pierre nodded. "We have to thank you, as well, for helping to rid us of a corrupt sheriff and a cruel overlord."

"Beauville will be a different place in the future," Edmund added, rising next to his brother.

"Aye, especially with our new sheriff," Pierre said, clapping Jean on the shoulder.

"Aye, I intend to crack down on all the rowdy bachelors in town and see that they get settled with proper wives," Jean joked.

Facing danger together had forged a bond among the nine men and the goodbyes were heartfelt, but finally Ranulf and Edmund were mounted on their horses and headed along the road to St. Gabriel.

"Does that finish up our business here?" Edmund asked. "We can be on our way to Lyonsbridge?" He said the words casually, but gave a sideways glance at his brother out of the corner of his eyes.

"I suppose," Ranulf answered with a scowl.

"Or was there anything else to be taken care of?" Edmund asked with feigned innocence.

"If you mean Bridget, she doesn't want me."

"Ah, forgive me. Somewhere along the line I missed the account of your meeting with her and, you know, the part where you told her that you loved her and that you wanted to spend the rest of your life with her because she was the only woman who has ever put that cowlike look in your eyes, with the possible exception of Diana, who, by the by, is *mine*. I missed that part," he ended.

Ranulf turned his head in astonishment. "You knew about my feelings for Diana?"

"Brother, for a smart man, you were ever a bit dim on the subject of women. All Lyonsbridge knew of your supposed feelings for Diana. But they weren't love. Think about it—if I had never come back, would you change your Bridget for Diana?"

"Not for an hour," he said immediately. Even the idea was preposterous. There was no comparison. Diana was beautiful, granted, but she was no more real to him than some kind of painting he could admire from afar. Whereas Bridget was more real than any woman he'd ever known. She was spirited and warm, innocent yet wise. She was everything he'd ever imagined in a partner. "Not for an instant," he said softly.

"So, it's too bad that even after hearing all these

wonderful sentiments on your part, the heartless woman turned you down.''

"I, well, she didn't turn me down, exactly.''

"Spurned you, then. Probably had you begging on your knees, too. Women are cruel that way."

Ranulf's grin was sheepish. "You know very well that I've not broached the subject."

"Ah, good. I always expect my women to be mind readers, as well. I think it only fair since their lovely bodies give them such an advantage over us oafish males."

Ranulf shook his head. "She says that all she wants is to settle back into life at the abbey and that she wishes none of us had ever come here."

Edmund stared at the dark road ahead of them. Finally he said, "I don't know why it's the *little* brother in our family who has to be giving all the advice, but I'll take on the task one more time. Women need to be told, Ran. They need to be loved and cajoled and courted and, above all, they need to be *told*."

They rode in silence for several minutes. Finally Ranulf said, "So you think I should tell her."

Edmund gave an exaggerated sigh. "Aye, brother, I do."

Once again the unaccustomed sound of a knock jolted her upright. She'd been lying in her bed for the past hour, but sleep would not come. Francis's story of her parents' love unto death and beyond kept running through her mind, mixed with unwanted thoughts of her encounter with Ranulf, here in this very bed.

She padded across the room in her bare feet and opened the door. Of course, it had to be him.

"Is it too late?" he asked, looking inside at the dark room. "I'm sorry, you were already sleeping."

She shook her head and stood back to allow him to enter. Then she moved to the bed and lit a candle. "Nay," she said. "Have you come to say goodbye? I thought you and your brother weren't leaving until morning."

He stepped into the room and carefully closed the door behind him. "I didn't come to say goodbye."

"Oh," she said. Now that the room was lit she felt a little self-conscious wearing only her thin shift. She sat on the bed and pulled the blanket up around her like a shawl.

"Are you cold?"

She shook her head.

He cleared his throat.

"What did you come for?" she asked finally.

He looked at her then with the particular look that told her exactly what he had come for, but she steeled herself to resist both the look and the memory it invoked.

"I came to tell you a story," he said, surprising her.

"At this hour?"

"Aye. The telling couldn't wait."

"Is it a long story?" she asked with a brief smile. She tucked her legs up underneath her on the bed and sat back, making herself comfortable, ready to listen.

Ranulf appeared to relax, also, as he grabbed her little stool and drew it up close to her cot. "Not too long. I was remembering that you liked to read stories in that library of yours."

Her voice grew soft. "Tales of adventure," she agreed. "Of knights and ladies."

"Tales of love," he added.

She nodded.

"Aye, I was remembering that you liked them, so I thought to myself, I'm going to tell Bridget a tale of a knight and the lady he loved."

"This may not be the time—"

He raised his hand. "It won't take long, I promise I'll skip all the once-upon-a-time stuff and just get to the part where the knight falls in love."

Bridget found herself focusing on the play of his smile around his lips as he talked. She gave herself a little shake and forced herself to pay attention. "The knight falls in love," she repeated.

"He *thinks* it's love," he amended. "But it's really not."

"Why not?"

"Because this lady actually belongs to someone else, and the only reason the knight thinks he loves her is because he's never found a woman he could love for himself."

Bridget leaned back against the wall.

"Don't fall asleep on me, now," Ranulf said. "I'm just getting to the good part."

"I'm not falling asleep," she said, working to keep her voice even when her entire insides seemed to be quaking.

"So then this knight, who'd always thought himself in love but never really had been, journeys to—" he paused "—a far-off land."

Bridget smiled. "To a magnificent castle?"

"Mmm...let's say to a magical place. And there he met a mysterious angel who saved his life."

"But he couldn't fall in love with an angel," Bridget said. "Because angels don't really live on earth."

"Ah, you're right. So let's say that the knight didn't *know* that it wasn't possible to fall in love with an angel, so he did anyway."

"Oh, dear. The poor knight."

"Exactly. For a long time he was rather miserable about it."

"And then what happened?" She was holding her hands clasped so tightly that the knuckles had grown white. He pulled his stool closer to the bed and reached out to gently separate them with his own hands.

"Then he turned her into a real woman," he said. His voice had grown hoarse.

"The knight did that?"

"Well, you see, it turns out that she actually *was* a real woman right from the start, so it all worked out."

"It did?"

He kicked the stool backward and moved to the bed, gathering her into his arms. "Aye," he said. "It did. It *will.*"

Then his mouth sought hers in a hungry kiss. "I love you, Bridget the angel," he murmured. "And I never want to be without you again. I don't care if we live at Lyonsbridge or Darmaux or St. Gabriel or in a cave somewhere. I want you by my side, and I want to make love to you every night and make lots of little baby angels with you."

Bridget laughed happily. "Baby angels?"

"Aye." He kissed her again, then let his hands caress her through the thin cloth of her shift. "Do you remember how it's done?"

"I'm not sure." She stretched to whisper directly into his ear, "You may have to give me another lesson."

"That's what I was hoping." Neither one had patience for lingering. It seemed as if his declaration had released a need that was only going to be filled when their bodies were merged. Clothes scattered and kisses turned to sighs and then shudders as they moved together in perfect union.

When it was over, they lay entwined, their heads side by side on a single pillow, staring into each other's eyes from just inches apart.

"You didn't finish the story," Bridget whispered.

"You've left me little energy for storytelling, sweetheart," he complained jokingly.

She smiled. "But I want to know what happened."

"To the knight and his angel?"

"Aye."

In the flickering candlelight, his blue eyes were brimming with love as he grinned and said, "Why, sweetheart, I thought you knew the ending. The knight and his angel lived happily ever after." Then he kissed her softly and rolled her back into his arms.

* * * * *

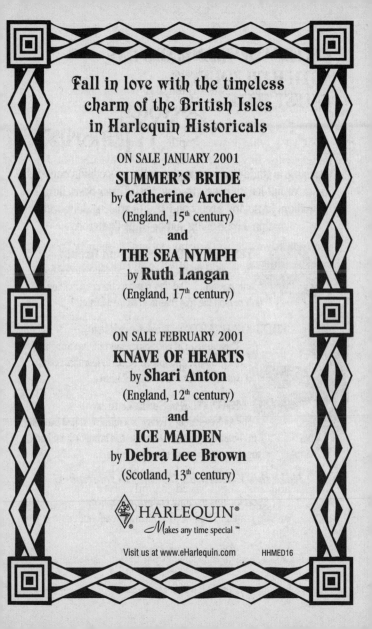

Fall in love with the timeless
charm of the British Isles
in Harlequin Historicals

ON SALE JANUARY 2001
SUMMER'S BRIDE
by **Catherine Archer**
(England, 15th century)
and
THE SEA NYMPH
by **Ruth Langan**
(England, 17th century)

ON SALE FEBRUARY 2001
KNAVE OF HEARTS
by **Shari Anton**
(England, 12th century)
and
ICE MAIDEN
by **Debra Lee Brown**
(Scotland, 13th century)

HARLEQUIN®
Makes any time special ™

Visit us at www.eHarlequin.com   HHMED16

CELEBRATE VALENTINE'S DAY WITH HARLEQUIN®'S LATEST TITLE— *Stolen Memories*

Available in trade-size format, this collector's edition contains three full-length novels by *New York Times* bestselling authors Jayne Ann Krentz and Tess Gerritsen, along with national bestselling author Stella Cameron.

TEST OF TIME by **Jayne Ann Krentz**—

He married for the best reason.... She married for the only reason.... Did they stand a chance at making the only reason the real reason to share a lifetime?

THIEF OF HEARTS by **Tess Gerritsen**—

Their distrust of each other was only as strong as their desire. And Jordan began to fear that Diana was more than just a thief of hearts.

MOONTIDE by **Stella Cameron**—

For Andrew, Greer's return is a miracle. It had broken his heart to let her go. Now fate has brought them back together. And he won't lose her again...

Make this Valentine's Day one to remember!

Look for this exciting collector's edition on sale January 2001 at your favorite retail outlet.

HARLEQUIN®
Makes any time special ™

Visit us at www.eHarlequin.com

PHSM

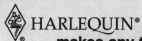

HARLEQUIN®
makes any time special—online...

eHARLEQUIN.com

shop eHarlequin

- ♥ Find all the new Harlequin releases at everyday great discounts.
- ♥ Try before you buy! Read an excerpt from the latest Harlequin novels.
- ♥ Write an online review and share your thoughts with others.

reading room

- ♥ Read our Internet exclusive daily and weekly online serials, or vote in our interactive novel.
- ♥ Talk to other readers about your favorite novels in our Reading Groups.
- ♥ Take our Choose-a-Book quiz to find the series that matches you!

authors' alcove

- ♥ Find out interesting tidbits and details about your favorite authors' lives, interests and writing habits.
- ♥ Ever dreamed of being an author? Enter our Writing Round Robin. The Winning Chapter will be published online! Or review our guidelines for submitting your novel.

Tyler Brides

It happened one weekend...

Quinn and Molly Spencer are delighted to accept three
bookings for their newly opened B&B, Breakfast Inn Bed,
located in America's favorite hometown, Tyler, Wisconsin.

But Gina Santori is anything but thrilled to discover her
best friend has tricked her into sharing a room with
the man who broke her heart eight years ago....

And Delia Mayhew can hardly believe that she's
gotten herself locked in the Breakfast Inn Bed
basement with the sexiest man in America.

Then there's Rebecca Salter. She's turned up at the
Inn in her wedding gown. Minus her groom.

*Come home to Tyler for three delightful novellas
by three of your favorite authors: Kristine Rolofson,
Heather MacAllister and Jacqueline Diamond.*

Take a trip to the Old West with four handsome heroes from Harlequin Historicals.

ON SALE JANUARY 2001

MAGGIE'S BEAU
by **Carolyn Davidson**

Beau Jackson, former soldier/rancher

and

BRIDE ON THE RUN
by **Elizabeth Lane**

Malachi Stone, ferry owner

ON SALE FEBRUARY 2001

SWEET ANNIE
by **Cheryl St.John**

Luke Carpenter, horseman

and

THE RANGER'S BRIDE
by **Laurie Grant**

Rede Smith, Texas Ranger

Harlequin® Historical

ANA SEYMOUR

has been a fan of English history since her childhood, when she devoured the historical epics of Thomas Costain, Rafael Sabatini and Anya Seton, and spent late nights up watching the swashbuckling movies of Errol Flynn and Tyrone Power. She spent a number of years working in the field of journalism, but she never forgot the magic of those tales. Now she is happy to be weaving some of that magic herself through Halrequin Historicals. Ana loves to hear from her readers at P.O. Box 24107, Minneapolis, MN 55424.

HHBIO540